T0065514

Fiercely Mine Forever

ENIOLA. F. FAGBEMI

authorHOUSE®

AuthorHouse™
1663 Liberty Drive
Bloomington, IN 47403
www.authorhouse.com
Phone: 833-262-8899

Published by AuthorHouse 03/26/2021

ISBN: 978-1-6655-1452-1 (sc)
ISBN: 978-1-6655-1451-4 (e)

Library of Congress Control Number: 2021901364

Print information available on the last page.

It's all fiction…

Dedication

To all the abiding love, perpetual sentiments,
fabricating affection to eternity.

H<small>E IS RESTFUL IN</small> his repose. Idle air drifts past his nostrils, his fatigued body aligned on a cluttered bed. For days, he ached for a snooze: a serene time he re-joins his shattered frame with a mystified mind. He anticipates treachery soaring in his existence, gets haunted by self-reproach and displeasure. In his restive seclusion, a part of him hails a looming victory while the other afflicts his heart terribly. He leans a jean clad leg on a bleached wall, drinking in its solace. Only a few steps away, over an unbolted door, a buoyant curtain clambers in slow progression, luxuriating a pleasant day. The atmosphere plays along. Dancing to every tune it plays, there's an outburst of a consuming breeze from the outdoors. Like a king dominating a throne, it takes up its spot leisurely, declining to a flowery end. Silence takes eminence in the room but for the recurrent sound of a laboring wall clock securing the surest glides of its second hand. It hurries through to catch up with the top of the hour. Once more, it makes a clean ascent of its flat surface adding, yet another minute.

Labi sits watching all around her. She hauls a long breath, rises to her feet. From the shadowy doorway, she shuffles across the room to a casement. She runs her magnificently manicured fingers on the parapet, staring blindly into space, mind fully subjugated with more trouble than she envisions. Her grieving eyes journey across the room to the position a snuffling sound infuses the air and back to the working clock. For the next forty seconds, she observes his bare flat belly mounting and descending then turns away sharply. It's a pretentious sleep, she admits. *Possibly to send me away.* She infers, darting him a contentious stare. She anticipates too much longer than she proposed to-too long for a genuine sleep. On her reading desk, in her hostel, lie five dissimilar projects, two of which are due for submission in twelve hours. An exhaustive study establishes a rewarding writing but there she stands lavishing her treasured time with a futile love.

She turns back again, flashes him a sad stare. No way out of the room until chapters of heart-rending worries distressing her brain are countered. Since his disclosure on her last visit, sleep has eluded her. She lays her head down to cogitate about her life, her tormented eyes always projecting the ceiling. The same old question resonates in her head, every time, anywhere.

Is Dayo really travelling out of the country or just kidding? He is playing one of his usual pranks, maybe. She breaks into a dull smile and saunters back to the entrance. Her hands tremble while she draws back the curtain swathed in draperies. The breeze is now more upsetting. It terrorizes the material, towering it in the air effortlessly. Labi moves further, unburdens its subduing attack, giving the door a slight push. She succeeds. It gets its freedom, for once since she arrived. Her heart sinks at the thought of reality. Who unburdens her heart from losing a beloved one? Who clears out the dust of defeat and treachery obscuring her conception and the mesh of distrust blinding her eyes of affection? If in due course, he forsakes her, life becomes worthless. Love itself is life. If broken, it is death-defying. She sighs heavily, suppressing the clog in her throat. Fear conquers her mind.

She knows that sentiment, has felt it thousands of times in her lifetime but this time, it's persuasive, damaging and pathetic. She feels it having a strong clutch at her heart, thrusting a frightful knife into her being. For a moment, she dreads psychosis, clashes with seclusion, even though he's still within her reach. Only in a couple of days, all her reflections about losing him to the new world will shape up, she estimates silently. And she will become a deserted lover reeling in the world of impracticalities.

He stirs in his sleep; she turns to look at him head-on. From the slumber, he wants more. He stretches his body, turns around and rests his head on his palm. He dozes off again. *For how much longer do I have to wait? Why can't he just tell me to go?* Trying to gulp back her plight, Labi is transfixed, her eyes dropped to the floor. She feels the weightiness of her heart pressuring her, nurtures an explosive perception internally. Everything has changed now, she knows. He doesn't give attention like before: no more cuddles, surprises, or assurances. He recently camped out in an imaginary friend's apartment for almost a week, then returned to sleep like a Koala. The only ally she knows with him rebuffs seeing him the previous day. She also discerned that he opts to be alone and treasure the thought of his glorious trip whenever she visits. Or make inevitable calls and arrangement behind closed doors and perhaps, hang out with his cousins. Although he's not compelled to unfold his strategies - the how and why of his whereabouts until they tie the knot. She agrees as he once forewarned her to watch her invasion in his private life. *That I know him doesn't give a chance to police him around or get in the way.* Agreed, but be that as it may, she needs a deep consideration of their love affair. Overall, he has proven to her that something is wrong. *That wrong I must know today.*

Labi stiffens with contempt. Her eyes travel to the frame glued to the wall. In it, she stands tucking her fists in a faded jean pocket, flashing a big smile at a camera. Dayo nuzzles up against her, wraps his arms around her, smiling. It's a portrait of love, an exposition of trust and loyalty. Where is that now? Where is the confidence she had in him to live through his trying times, when he recently purports to leave her all by herself and hanker after money? To her, that's not the true definition of love. He is simply the bane of her life. She smiles faintly and sighs at the thought of a new development. If truly it's the way love goes, she regrets. Deep within her heart, she boils and gets fiercely plagued by an unstable feeling. She needs help turning back the hands of time, making him do everything he used to do in the past when their affair just fired up. He will settle for her like before. She feels like a part of her is ripping off.

Now, he barely spends thirty minutes without nit-picking or projecting to go elsewhere. He's always on the move to get this done or get that fixed. In particular, she's not being loved back as expected. And that's the reason he must awake from his sleep and answer thousands of questions fretting her mind, giving her sleepless nights and worrisome days. He is obliged to confess his true sentiments for her recently. Labi sniffs, pulls back the tears in her eyes. She puffs, gasps again and again.

She casts a wary look at him for a moment, speculating, musing on what action to take against him to keep him by her side forever. She recently gathered a lot of disheartening reports about distant relationships. It doesn't ever work for both partners, especially when another woman is involved. Out of sight is truly out of mind, except by divine mediation. But come what may, she prepares to work it out with him.

At a snail's pace, she approaches him on the bed. He is still in a deep sleep, must have spent his whole night tunneling in some issues she knows nothing about. Now, she deals with a strange man in a new life. With considerable frustration, she stoops to tap him awake. What is worth doing needs deliberation at the right time.

'I'm returning to my hostel. Aren't you tired of sleeping? If you're tired of seeing me here, please ask me to leave. That's better than faking an endless and pretentious sleep', she gives him a bad eye, shoves his legs to sit on the border of the bed. He opens his blood-shot eyes, looks straight at her. For seconds, he marshals his mind into reality. He remembers, she laid beside him and he did his utmost to drive her to sleep too. What happened next? Did she sleep at all? He tries to summon up more, battling with his memory lane. As he hoists himself with an elbow, a vital part of their last dialogue relapses. He remembers her numerous questions on his projected trip and their relationship. In three seconds, he also recollects promising to talk to her when he awoke. It ultimately dawns on him that the hour has arrived to hand in a needless confession. He holds his throbbing head and falls back in bed. The previous night was too busy for him: much love and excitement he wished had lasted past this decisive time he is being probed by his supposed hindrance.

'You told me you will sleep for only twenty minutes. You asked for just twenty minutes and now- look at the time'. They both stare at the clock concurrently. It's six pm. She ought to leave and complete her tasks, nonetheless she doesn't care. Lately, she knows, her nervousness borders only on her love affair. Too bad for her studies, she knows but she loves Dayo so much. Much more than her life.

He looks around the room, half awaken-half confused, still in the sub conscious. He realized, at the moment, that he is actually in his room, lying close to his traumatized half. He shot her a straight look, sighs and rolls on his side. For the next two minutes, they are both silent. Silent but the sound of the clock habitually ticking and Labi's disconcerted legs pivoting more frequently than the clock. They move sideward in deep thought. His transgression generates more gravitational attraction, awakes an unrepressed tide about to break out. She wants to talk, pour out all the fusses in her mind and get a lot of relieve.

Where will she start from? From where their conversation last ended. He only explained how he got help from a female friend to study in America. *Who is she?* He swore she is a friend, but she isn't foolish to buy into that certitude. No one can hoodwink her at that age, that a mere lady- friend will offer him bursary abroad with no string attached. Its utterly out of the question in this computer age. There's certainly something he has to give in return: something akin to love or marriage. She pulls a perceptible sigh, then turns around to face him squarely.

'Dayo- you still haven't explained to me who this your messiah is. Is she a kind of heavenly sister or what? I don't understand. Can you make this clear to me?', she expects an answer, looking in a different direction, an attentive ear reaching him. He rubs his palm over his face, winks an eye lash off his tingling sight. Setting his feet to the floor, just next to her, he awkwardly scratches his head. He feels itchy around her, meditating a new version of a persuasive lie to tell. She turns so infuriating for her immoderate curiosity. He still can't admit how their relationship hovered to the stage of prying into each other's affair. He hasn't accepted her wholly, to plough into his private life. *I will never let you break the barrier, no matter what. I'm still free to live my life the way I want.*

However, she wants much more than that. She needs to know him inside-out.

'Dayo-did you just hear me? You haven't-',

'She's just a friend', he breaks in, snapping. There is an expression of shock on her face. He discerns this, then slows down a little bit. He breaths inconvenience. If only he knew she was going to catch him there, he would have wielded his ploy - possibly vanish in the city and hang out with friends. Nevertheless, he is inclined to explain and never cease to explain the basis of his trip.

'Labi', he tries to control his voice and temper. Knowing how soft she is on the inside; he chooses to put the situation under control. His mind reflects a thousand and five requests at once. But most of all, he needs time away from her, to thoughtfully plan his transition into a new life in a new world.

'Labi', he pulls closer, swathes a demonstrative arm

around her, his beard sweeping her lustrous face. She begins to revel in the passion of a deprived love she longed for. Her body lightens up, she senses a log of wood trundling off her heart. Her thirsts for love heighten, she wants to be there forever and never asked for anything else except that one love in his protective arms. Next to no time, she is enthralled. She watches his compulsive effect engulf her willful ego. Her arm reaches for him- a little bit around his loin then plunges back tiredly. Just as he presumes, she is abruptly joggled by an impulse and she gets back to her senses. She retracts in gradual process, her body inclining back to its position of admiration and ideals. He knew she wouldn't fall for that, with all her endowed elegance, but he would do his best possible. With a cynical smile playing around his lips, he whispers to her implacably, 'my love, that lady is only my helper and nothing else. That's it, believe me. I can't ever betray you'. He believes, he must have said it all well, even though she doesn't give in to his desire.

'Besides, if not for the chat you saw on my phone, you wouldn't have a clue about this', he adds, rousing her temper.

'How do you mean?', she flashes him a hard stare, dropping his arm from her shoulder. Did that make any sense to her? Is he kidding her? She is infuriated, her thunderous mien takes the stand. She acknowledges that the longer she stays there, the more he drives her crazy.

'I mean- it's not what you should know. It causes- jeal-jealousy as you portray right now. And- there's sincerely nothing between us'. He rolls his eyes tiredly.

'Oh really? Are you for real? I shouldn't be concerned

about a lady taking you away to God- knows- where in the name of assistance, right?', she gnashes her teeth, arch her fingers in portrayal of absurdity. Now dazed by fury and irritation, she breaks off to shake her head then darts him a vengeful look. If a deduced love like theirs crashes, then she doesn't believe in true love. She concludes, turning her gaze away from him gruffly. Not up to ten seconds, another question storms her mind and she turns to him. It is indeed an opportunity to give vent to her spiteful sentiments.

'Let me ask you a question. What do you take our relationship for? A joke? Is it a joke that I've been with you for six years and you think- ', she reserves the heart-splitting comment she is about to make. Her voice rises from medium to an infuriating high pitch. She rants and raves, it fills the air. When he opens his mouth to lull her, she raises an arm to stop him.

'Listen to me. Now is the time you tell me what this is all about. Are you dumping me here to follow someone richer and more helpful?', she breathes hard, looks vindictive. At this point, Dayo sees what is coming. He drops his legs back on the floor, wraps his arms around himself. His head drops in contemplation of what to say or do to put off her burning emotion. For the first time, he watches her ego with deep surprise- the personality he hasn't seen since they met. Things are quite out of hands, and he accepts his self-reproach, however he will never change his mind.

'Labi', he unclogs his throat to be perceptible. 'You have to believe me. That lady is only a friend. I repeat-she is just a friend. I mean, how many times do you need me to repeat that? She just wants to help me and that is it. There's nothing more- that's it', he replies bluntly. He grows angry too but allows his conscience to reach a decision. She listens without disrupting, her throbbing head merely buried in her hands. By the time she raises her face, she decides to take her leave before she goes wild. She can't predict what their argument would lead to, even when she knows he hasn't proposed to her or walked her down the aisle. He is free to make his choices right now. *I have to go.*

'Okay- fine. I've heard you'. She rises from the bed, begins to look around for her disarrayed stuffs in the room. On every occasion she visits, they find various convenient spots. First, she found her watch under his pillow, then a decorative scarf and a pair of sneakers next to his desk. Her eyes fall on her cuff bangles sitting next to a leather bag he recently gifted to her. While she looks around for her textbooks, she feels a fierce clutch around her wrist. She fidgets to break free, looking down at only his grip. She envisages this, knows him so well with his sequence of actions. He's always so loving and caring.

'Labi, stop this. Stop! Stop frustrating yourself. Be wise at this time'. He gets tired of her persistence, snatches her shoes from her and tosses them at the door. Her eyes follow the same direction in surprise, the second pair alighting on its duo in rapid succession. She knows he is angry and not pleased about their present situation.

'Look, do you think I'm foolish? Do you think I'll love to marry you in penury and share this my naked mattress with you in matrimony? Come on, don't be stupid. When there's a will, there's always a way. I have to make moves to- '.

'Marry a rich lady to settle with me? What will be my position?'

'Shut up! Labi, shut up. If you don't want to listen, for all that I care, do as you wish'. He gets so infuriated. No matter what, he believes she isn't in position to misjudge his struggles to excel in life. He drops her arm, then picks the shoes from the door. He hands them over.

'Take your shoes. You may leave if you want to. We shall discuss this when you're ready'. At the point she senses her strength sinking, she relaxes. She collects her shoes, sits down quietly and wears them one after the other, with noticeably trembling hands. By the time she's done, he's also ready to leave the room. From the corner of her eyes, she watches him fasten the last two buttons in his shirt, looking away sternly. She realizes he already made up his mind about his decision. Come rain or shine, nothing stops him. She takes her bag in silence, takes two slow steps approaching him at the door. She faces him and says with a wobbly voice, 'Dayo- remember the implication of what you're about to do. Remember we had a covenant to strengthen our love. You can't marry someone else and I can't'. She holds back the tears in her eyes.

'I know darling-I know that I'm yours forever and you're mine forever. But that oath doesn't stop me from accepting offers from friends, does it? I have to take steps forward in my life'.

'Okay-I get you. I got everything you said. I have to leave now. I have to go'. She pushes the door open. It's been a bad long day for her dawdling from issue to issue. He seems too difficult and unbending with his rigid decision. Another day, maybe. The conversation isn't over until he draws a line. When she pulls the door open to leave, she feels a restraining hand around her elbow. She turns around to receive a startling kiss on her lips.

She cleaves to her bag, braces her body, struggles to break free from him and -just leave the room. He holds still, didn't let go until she surrenders to his passion. Two hearts found a ritual trail and get allied once again. For the moment he's still around, everything remains the same even her defeated convictions. But for the truth that already unfurls, that there is a sure fire. Is he still hers forever or just a façade? Will the bond between them still hold after his departure? Tens of questions reverberate in her head, even in her moment of affection.

2

'I PLANNED TO VISIT BY ten. I wanted to surprise you', Segun fills an ornamental glass cup with ice-cold water. He keeps his eyes on it to the brim, the angle of his sight on his attentive friend. They both concentrate to its uppermost point, breathing glee and realization for coming together again.

'Fill the back too', Dayo jokes as he crowns the bottle and returns it to the fridge, beaming. It's been a while since he set his eyes on him. For a couple of weeks now, they've been chatting only on phone, unlike their pretty closest time together. Or when they lived in the same apartment and grew in the same neighborhood. And they got too close to tell almost everything about each other. Segun is an ear to his head. Too close, more than a mere friend.

He saunters to his home bar, looks around at a line of liquor. His brand is always spirit. He is not into wine. He peers over his shoulder and asks, 'hey man, you want something to drink?'

Dayo leans over the arm of a white fleecy sofa, giggling. 'No- nothing on top of this water'. Holding up his glass, he adds, 'thank you though'.

'You are welcome, anytime'. He takes a leisurely walk

back to the living room, his usual cordial smile still lingering on his face. The twilight glances through a knotted curtain in the room, reminds him of someone. Then his eyes travel up a large silvery clock gliding down the hour of seven- two hours past the projected time. He drops his hands resignedly, and proceeds into the room. It never crossed his mind till he arrived. He has spent the past four hours working on his computer, forgetting a commitment.

'How are you doing?', Dayo draws his attention back to the room, surveying his strange behavior.

'Fine, my man. I'm glad you're here'. He breaks into a broad smile, still wondering why there's a delay. Finally, he captures his attention. He looks around for a suitable spot to sit.

Since his proposition to travel overseas, he lessened the number of times they meet in months. Only telephones safeguard incessant ties with habitual conversation about love and life. Packing up his computer, he recalls their last chat about his duple love affair. It took him about an hour to dissuade him to no avail. They hadn't enough time to discuss how he muddles through. *And now is the time.*

He reoccupies his position on an adjacent couch, watching him guzzle the whole content. He sits the cup on a center table, near a synthetic flower vase when he is done.

'The Day of O- the Day of O', he calls him fondly, laughing from ear to ear. He stretches his tired legs, then focuses on him. He reminisces all his undertakings to flee Africa in every way possible and laughs silently.

To him, the continent is not so unpleasant to be deserted like everyone does- home is home. *Besides, if we all choose to leave, who stays to fix the plaguing political, social, economic and health issues we have around. If the whites left their countries, there wouldn't be luring development today. Let's think about this.* He believes he does so well in his enterprise and is gratified with his little but satisfactory earnings. In no time is he geared up to get into the distress of journeying to a strange continent where there is no family or friends but a tread on a thin line between home and abroad. In such places, you have indistinct placement in the society unlike your usual life, not much recognition is accorded. He stoops to a slave yearning for the crown- plausible impossibilities. What can he do without his family whose doors are opened to his desires at all costs, in good faith? Everything is like chancing his luck in the hands of a familial opportunist, so he chooses liberty and satisfaction in his home continent.

Notwithstanding, he merits his sheer admiration and reassurance for a crowned determination. It comes to past that he will be departing soon. He surely stands a chance to rise higher than his folks but is he mindful of all the concerns and hurdles involved? He has heard success stories of people taking the bull by the horn and making their fortunes and the disasters of thousands of disheartened immigrants. Life may be so disappointing there but since he made up his mind, he will be happy to support his bravery. The same bravery he wielded since their childhood- to get the best result amongst his peers and outshine in every group work. He knows he will make it there; his will reveal efficacious stories. He feels happy for him always and ever in the spirit of good friendship. He always makes him proud.

Segun rises to prepare a meal for them to eat as he recalls his expectation that night, once more. He breaks into a cloudy smile crossing his ally's legs to the kitchen. He thinks he heard him say something. He pauses to listen again and catches him talking to a television host, disparaging a thorny reality show. He gives no reply in his moodiness, merely set their salad in a tray, then returns to the room.

In the coolness of the night, the two inseparable friends are occupied with different thoughts- one pondering on his glorious trip abroad and the other ruminating about his newly found love. They have conversed too often in their friendship that there is nothing new to discuss, except there is a new development. As if reading each other's mind, Segun diverts his attention to his upcoming plans, considering how much he will miss him.

'When are you travelling abroad? What date is on your flight ticket?', he jolts him a little bit. He was actually thinking of how to see Meghan and shop with her as planned. They have only two weeks to tour around and also get all the items needed for their proposed wedding at a cheaper rate.

'Man-I have only two weeks here. I have to see you every time now. And that's the reason I'm here', he picks up a television controller, begins to search for pleasurable networks. He pushes to his favorite reality show and stops. He relaxes in the sofa, legs straightened on the center table.

Segun's mind wanders to Labi at the moment. She is relevant, has been the only one he knew with him for six years. When Meghan occurred in his life, he had no control over him, even though he spoke of her often. He leans forward to speak about her again.

'What about Labi? How is she coping with this situation?'

'I don't know. I've explained everything to her, but she doesn't want to admit -that our relationship remains the same'.

Segun gives him a knowing look and asks, 'does she know that you are going to marry Meghan abroad? Did you make her understand what is at stake?'

'Segun, there is no time in the world she will accept another woman in my life. This is Labi we are talking about, remember? I only told her she is my helper and that's it'.

'And- you think she is stupid to accept?', he cocks his head in a direction.

'Well', he shrugs, picks the remote to change the channel. He feels irrefutably perturbed discussing her issues. His decision has a lot to do with his progress. He doesn't care what she feels right now if their differences can be resolved in the future. But first thing comes first. He can't trade his luck for her love.

Knowing how difficult the conversation has always been, Segun switches to a different subject that may interest him.

'Are you sleeping here tonight?'

'Hmm, I don't know. What about Soronje?', he gives his mind to his girlfriend- a trained talker who a parrot will never equal in loquacity.

'You will sleep in the guest room'. He looks in the direction of a private room in a corner of his apartment, tries to distract him from discussing her verbosity. Without delay, he switches back to his own topic.

'Dayo- you know ladies so well. She won't wait for you.

She will begin a new affair if you stay for too long. She is a big fish'. He says pointedly.

'Anyways, if that happens, then I will be happy as a dog with two tails. Happy to let me off the hook'. He rises from his seat and paces around the room. God knows how much discomfort he gets from their conversation. The thought of Labi makes his heart boggle- he feels guilty every now and then. He is simply at a loss, what to do to resolve the dilemma: travelling out of the country to make money or giving the thought a miss and remain with the lion in his way. However, what matters at present is money and power, not love. On the whole, he is primed.

Segun looks outside through the window and back in the house. He has passed his side unknowingly and now he stands next to a glass window, the curtain in splits. This is all about a lady he never admitted that he loves. One mention about his love sparks off agitation, rouses anger and hatred. If that is the true situation, Dayo wonders why he is so disconcerted in her absence. Without being told, he knows he expects her terribly. This is proven in the next two seconds.

'I wonder why this lady is not back yet. Why is she out till this time?', he looks at the time, drops his arm and looks outside again. He sees people still moving around the neighborhood but no trace of her approaching. Dayo giggles. *You can't be serious man. Are you kidding me?*

'Who?', Dayo sinks in the same sofa, pretending not to know his direction.

'Soronje, of course'.

He seizes the opportunity to talk about his relationship and never mention Labi anymore, if possible.

'Eh, do you want to marry this girl?'.

'Never! She is an idle talker. I'm only trying to keep her safe', a quizzical smile plays around his lips. Is that true? Maybe, maybe not. He is getting to like her for her striking caring actions, and ardor even though he has no plan, whatsoever to settle with her. But something about her draws him closer. He thinks she isn't as bad as she appears to be. Friends and family haven't yet accepted her except she changes her talking habit. Her loquacity turns people off her geniality, perhaps. Still, he believes in himself so well. There will always be someone around to stir him from his slumber when he tries to marry her out of pity.

'Really? Are you sure?', Dayo asks sarcastically. With that, he conceded that Soronje is never a lady of honor. She is a blotch on his white garb- a blot he must wipe out whichever way. When he was with Barbara, his ex-girlfriend, there was never a thing like that. They were both respected. It was never a one-sided respect. With her, it is different. For her unsought conversations, she turns an object of ridicule.

'It seems you enjoy every bit of her company. You have been anticipating her arrival. You are in love with her- and you keep denying. Friend, be careful what you do', he warns with a beady side- eye. He thinks she is a low life. Only people like that talk nineteen to the dozen, the rich do not.

'Oh no- that can never happen'. He rejoinders, displeased with his ally's overmuch pressure and joke. He must end the joke. Recently, he can't deny having a stronger feeling for her but for her bad habit. If only she could turn a new leaf, he would settle with her.

'She talks too much'. He emphasizes with a strong nod, almost throwing off his head. With that, he gets even with him.

First, he wanted to talk about Labi and quieten him but had a diversion for something more important he must know.

'But-she is still better than some ladies that don't talk at all. They are no fun at all. No matter what you say, they remain mute like a lonely ghost. Just that- ', he speaks in her defense. Again, Dayo marks this as a sign of affection. He is, indeed, in love with her. It's unbelievable that Segun has finally fallen in her hands despite all his efforts. Barbara, Soronje, Janet or whoever he has seen with him before is never his perfect match. He often settles for the less privileged. On one side of him, he thanks his lucky star for rising up higher, lucky to associate with a supportive lover. If that is what he wants from life, he wants to play along to gladden him at this point. He wants his joy.

'Come off it. Those ones are sick upstairs. She is better than them'. Dayo takes the controller again to search for something different. He needs to stop prying in his privacy and mind his business. It's his life, anyway. He doesn't look in his way, but he feels his sudden change of mood. He remains as cool as cucumber.

That he harbors such a woman has always been a course for concern. He has considered deserting her thousands of times however, it's never actualized. He met her two years ago in her supermarket; a strong, industrious, hardworking and determined lady. All her good values overshadow a mere loquacity, so he doesn't actually care much about that. And this is why he keeps her, hoping for a change one day.

'What's happening outside?', Dayo reduces the volume of the television, and pays attention. At the same time, both friends cock their heads to listen.

'In fact, there were so many people at the bus station, and I wonder if they will get home tonight. About eighty people waiting to join just one bus. And guess what happened to a woman in the crowd. While she waits impatiently for the bus- ', the speaker drops the handbag hanging loosely on her shoulder and continues, 'a boy accidentally knocks off her wig and her rotten head got exposed. Oh God- no one would have known what this woman hides under that wig. It looked horrible- she looked horrible'. She pauses, laughs and begins to talk again. Her listener is straight-faced.

'At the same time, a dog emerged and chased everyone away. I quickly grabbed my stuff and went into hiding. A dog's bite is a disease, you know?' she laughs and begins a new topic.

'You know the last time I didn't end the story of my friend that plans to divorce her hubby because of his gluttony. Me Soronje, I will never leave my love. True love is hard to find. You see, Segun is mine forever and nothing changes that, I swear', she touches her tongue and points at the sky, swears by the moon and the stars.

Both friends listen on, Segun's head lowered sadly.

'Wonderful-hmm', the listener's disinterested voice is heard for the first time. Only her kid's aspirin brought her out of her apartment to encounter a verbal diarrhea. 'Have a good night'. She closes her door to attend to the kid. For a moment, she stands smiling, unhappy about her inactive contribution to limitless topics. From number one to the last, still the same. Must be a confirmed sadist. She vows never to talk to her next time; gives her door a bad eye then turns back to leave.

Dayo and his friend exchange glances. People make choices in life to achieve a goal. Knowing his heavenly brother chooses a woman for a reason he doesn't wish to disclose to him or anyone, he reserves his comment.

His usual reaction reflects his predetermined impression that she is the best for him, so what's his stress? He sneaks a look at him, smiles and looks away. They both deciphered Soronje's voice and he's not going to comment about her first, right before her beloved.

'You see? That is what I mean- imagine such a woman giving five detailed stories in just five minutes. She talks too much and that's her only problem', he says to Dayo's surprise. He spreads five fingers in his face angrily, 'five! Five whole stories. I'm in soup'.

'Five? Was it up to five?', he asked chuckling. He takes his time to study his mood. He appears utterly disappointed in her, seems to have fallen in love except for her incorrigible flaws. If only he could fix that, he sincerely loves her.

'Tell me how I can settle with someone like that even if I want to', he reveals finally. 'She talks too much, too much that her neighbor walked away'.

Dayo pauses for a moment, now paying attention to how he can resolve his problem rather than his unending complaint about her. There should be a way forward.

'You know, Segun- you can actually change her. You can bend her to your taste. That's how she can be yours forever', he advices, placing much noticeable emphasis on forever.

'That's not a good advice. I don't worry about that. I have to retire inside before she- ', he prepares to disappear into his room and avoid her. This isn't good enough.

'Stop being like that. You will- at least- stay and open the door -else she will think I'm influencing you'. He rose to his six feet and rather makes his way to the guest room, same place he sleeps whenever he visits. Segun sits back in the sofa, heeding to his advice unhappily. He grabs the controller where he dropped it and tunes to almost all the channels available, yet has no choice. Everything is as tasteless as Soronje. He wishes she had somewhere else to go but impossible. He threw the controller on the table.

The bell begins to ring shortly. She presses it five different times, yet no one answers from the inside. She hears the tv set, feels the liveliness in the apartment, then leans over to peer through the door. Right on the couch, next to the tv, she sees Segun watching a programme, crossing his legs, and relaxing like there was no sound at all. This enrages her. She presses the bell continuously, places her finger on it ceaselessly.

'Honey, its Soronje. Come and open the door. Why are you sitting there like a statue?', she grabs the door, shakes it really hard.

'Be careful. My neighbors are sleeping', he rises from his seat, opens the door quickly and runs into his room. The door slams after him in a jiffy. Her mouth hangs open in surprise. What on earth is wrong with him? Something is obviously wrong, but it never struck her that it has anything to do with her expression of joy. God knows the delight she gets from talking to people and pouring out her heart. A day without any conversation makes her sick. It is her way, her joy he must love to accept if they will live happily ever after.

'And where are you running to? What is your problem?'. Her eyes hang around the direction he took. She drops the bulk she carries and sinks in the sofa to relax her legs, still shocked at the inhospitable treatment she received from him. Whenever she visits, she expects the best treatment from a beloved one, not deception and malice. On the whole, something would have prompted his reaction. She doesn't know what bothers him, was precisely in the dark. *Oh God almighty, what else will I do to please this man? There is nothing I haven't done to please him; he is still unhappy. I bet God made him in unhappy times'.*

She gathers her stuff together; makes her way to the same room he retires for a reason he needs to explain. *Whether you like it or not, you are fiercely mine forever.*

3

I TS PITCH DARK. COOL gust of air grooms her velvety face whilst she plunges in her bag for a cluster of keys. Its inaccessible, even at the bottom. She thrusts a demanding hand in the central pouch where all essentials are kept, yet not within reach. She is perplexed. Only in seconds, the bag is descended from her shoulder to the bare floor for a meticulous hunt. Not a single light at the patio, but her obliging phone torch gazing in corners to fish it out. She spots it lounging and glistening in the belly pocket, then clutches it with a start to unlock the door. With only two sharp-witted turns, it opens. A cracking sound breaks the silence of the night. It moves rearward, towards the hindmost, where it habitually retires for a break. She advances towards it, marshals it back to its lock to keep safe from every menace prowling around- from the known and unknown. Since she returned from America, she's been tremendously on her guard, bearing in mind every daunting news she gathered about the hoodlums in her neighborhood. Being a foreigner is another cause for concern: the major reason for her heightened anxiety

She is the one in custody of hard currency, the

presumed most haunted at the moment. Before heading into her bedroom, she twists the doorknob to be sure.

She feels comforted stepping down from an exquisite hill of fashion she mounted all day. Her toes feel healthier, glad to sing praises of their openness since 5am. Now they breath better, their physical space reinstated. The early hours flew by with frantic schedules for her proposed trip back home with her dearest. There were vital documentations in the past two years and finally they triumph to the final stage after his visa was granted. The rest of the process continues in America when they both get legally married.

It's not been easy so far. She is ultimately over the moon having a seal of approval. For the past four years, she has been with only her pet, Kish- not a boyfriend or hubby. And now, Dayo returns with her to perfect her. Like magic, he came into sight on a social media platform. It's amazing he hails from the same country and state as her mother. By force of circumstances, her parents got separated when she was precisely six. Where did she belong afterwards? Her African-American father restrained her from returning home with her African mother and two other siblings, amidst chaos. Following the court rulings, in her interest, she has the choice to stay back. Was this good for her? Yes, to an extent, she admitted to it that, it was the best decision she took in her life, except for the motherly love she didn't get as a kid. On the other hand, her two sisters are particularly poles apart in culture and socialization. Despite her root in the continent, she hasn't, for once, lived there like her other siblings. Dayo realizes her aspiration to hook up with her estranged family.

So far, so well, Dayo is the best of all the men she has

met. He's nice, adorable, god- fearing and of course, sexy. He completes all her needs in a man. In her early thirties, when she thinks she is getting out of shape and luckless, she is going to flaunt her younger spouse to all her loathsome friends and enemies looking down upon her. *America, here we come. I am the best, so I got the best. Let y'all bring out your hubby and let's see whose is the best. I have seen them all before, so they can't win in this contest. Mine is the best and he's mine forever. All those husband snatchers wriggling in skimpy and slinky shorts. Y'all back off! I aint kidding with my man.*

The nauseating thought of Sarah crosses her mind as she opens the refrigerator to get a chilly drink. She is a favorite friend that has a weakness to seduce married men and displace wives. Not quite long ago, two of her close friends fell her victims and now she prepares to snub her. *Seriously, from now on, she's not my friend. I'ma wring life out of that bitch if she crosses my path. I need no friend at this time. Just me and my boo-boo and that's it- that's what I need. That's it.* She closes her eyes against the thought, shakes her head and reaches for her phone. She sees a list of missed calls from her sister, mother and father in America, not a call from Dayo. What happened? Why not a call from him after he left her apartment the previous night? She remembers she has called his number several times without a response. He earlier explained why he needed to spend time with an old friend and the next two days with his parents in the outskirt of the city. Is everything alright?

In melancholy atmosphere, she sinks in the sofa next to her bed, begins to leaf through her phone, her cheerless eyes exploring all previous calls. She glues the I-phone to her ears awaiting a quick response. He probably didn't want to bother her safe- drive home or got tied up with his folks. It rings on, yet no response. She switches from ear to ear, takes off her hoop ear rings with a feeling of apprehension. Without noticing, she begins to fidget. Her mind lingers on what he is doing at the moment: whatever thwarts her need for attention. Over time, she's been trained to trust him, and she does. But what is wrong at the moment? Could he be watching soccer in the bosom of his friends' room or deeply asleep? Her eyes flies to a golden wall clock on the wall. It is past ten. He can't sleep that early, especially with a friend that absorbs him with much more conversation. But wherever he is, she acutely anticipates his baritone voice.

'Hello?' a feminine voice surfaces from the end.

She is shocked, a sudden chill sweeps through her. Meghan clears her throat, sits up in her bed, her heart beating rapidly.

'Hello? Please who am I speaking with?', she blinks, clears her throat.

'I should be the one asking you that question because you called me'. The voice appears with more growing annoyance. Her heart beats faster. She rises from the sofa, begins to tread around the room. *Rude. This is serious. Who the hell is this?*

'What can I do for you? If it's a wrong number, please get off my phone'. The respondent hangs up on her.

Oh my God, oh my God. what was that? Who on earth was that on his phone, with his number? Did I call a wrong number? She looks down at the number registered on her phone if there was an error. No, there wasn't a mix-up, it's under 'my love' in her contact. *That may be the wrong person with the right number.* With a sinking heart, she takes a break, ruminating over her next reaction. She grabs her pillow closer, tucks it under her braided hair. Her mentality exploits unforeseen circumstances leading to lack of trust and possibly the end of their relationship as it happened with her exes. She swallows hard, sneaks a look at her phone in deep surprise. What next? Will she sit, fold her arms and watch the phone as if it committed an offence or find out who received the call? To prevent this from happening, she built the impulse to manage unpleasant situations in their courtship. However, she isn't sure who it was. *Was that his ex-love he once told me about or another one. Was that his only sister? No, that cannot be, I know her voice. Or was his phone stolen?* Not sure about the condition, she develops a second thought. She calls up his number again.

'Yes? Are you back?', the voice gets very harsh and rude.

'Who are you? Please give the phone to the owner. I want to speak to him. Is Dayo there with you?' she requests politely, wonders what her reaction would be.

'Hmm- such a polite request. But sorry-you can't speak with him tonight because he's here in my cool embrace. He keeps saying that he doesn't want to speak to anyone. He is not ready to talk to anyone', she laughs in her frustration.

'Girl- you've been crazy from your cradle. Do you know who you are dealing with? Return the phone if its stolen', she says out of breath, summoning the trust she has in him.

'And what will be your reaction if you spot him right here, next to me? Go to bed- girl. He is mine- forever. And steer clear forever. Else-' she laughs again, roars with laughter.

Meghan switches off her phone, throws it away. She watches its last rebound before vaulting in the angle of her bed. There is a breathless air in the room. She rushes to push her windows open. It's very dark outside, yet there is power outage. But for her antique white battery powered lamp, she would be in the dark too. She pushes her face out for fresh air, allows it to permeate her being for a while.

She huffs for a couple of minutes, struggling with the effect of her emotive encounter. The impulsive conversation, patently, marks the culmination of his betrayal and mistrust in their relationship. He never, for once, confirmed that he returned to his ex-girlfriend after his refutation of her premature break off- as he narrated to her in the beginning. He swore not to return to her even though she apologizes repeatedly for her heart-breaking behavior. While she knows he lies, she confides in him with a challenging resignation.

She gives a long- long sigh, stretches her body on her cozy bed, her eyes projecting the ceiling. It's her shower time but she can't. She must reach the bottom of her problem, re-claim her peace of mind before settling in. *What have I gotten myself into? Oh my God, won't this man betray me in America? Will our marriage last forever? I hope he's not just using me to enter United states and desert me afterwards. And isn't it too late now?* So risky, she thinks. Discretion is the better part of valor. Her sister often lays prominence on this expression whenever she seeks her opinion. But witty words are well utilized by their users in true life situations. She knows quite a lot about the men in their domain, unlike her that travelled all the way down to gamble for a heart. She has managed her marriage for twelve years now and is still in it. *How possible?* She wonders all the time. To attain a purposeful result, she has tremendously assisted her in her own way, from the beginning till now. Five years now, she has been her mainstay, has always been there. For her assurance alone, she learnt to accept and trust her relationship. Altogether, she has sincerely lent a hand to push it this far. Should she be left out at this tough time at all? No, she needs her consolation and assurance to remain in the affair.

She crawls to the edge of her bed in search of her phone. It went further than she expected. Two missed calls now display on the screen. *Did he call back?* She rushes to check. It was Anthony, another admirer she will not accept in her life. Only Dayo's call will terminate her malaise at the moment, not an annoying, uninviting buffoon. She murmurs beneath a weary breath as her fingers search for a contact.

'Hello- Mercy', she swallows her sob stuff.

'Hey sis. How are you doing?', a hearty voice comes from the end.

'Not okay at all. I'm not feeling well. I should have driven to your house right now but for the danger on the way at this time', she closes her eyes in distress.

'Are you serious? Look- you can't get here at this time. Tell me, what happened?' she pays attention to her.

'Mercy, look-I'm tired of this whole situation. I am really tired-really-really tired', she holds back the tears in her eyes.

'What happened between you and your fiancé? Have you seen him today?', she fishes for information, imagines what her problem could be. There would possibly not be something else except her love affair.

'I called him when I just returned home and

to my surprise, a lady answered his call. Can you believe this? And she was so rude to me- very rude. So rude- nasty- stupid- savage'.

Mercy breaks into a smile. To her, it means nothing. She has far too much of experience about marriage and disappointment. It's not a big deal. Once again, she draws a long breath then said in a low, pacifying tone, 'Dayo is not like that. I trust him so well; he can't give his phone to a lady to insult you- his wife- to- be. You are his wife. Come on Meghan don't be childish. That may be his sister pranking you. It's our way here'.

'Prank? Did you just say prank? Try to get me right. She confirmed that she is his lover- that-', she attempts creating an illusion of her unknown, war-ridden foe, coiling up in a bikini, next to him in a soft luxurious bed and expecting another call from her. She closes her eyes in pain.

'Meghan. Come on, you don't live here with us, do you? They may try to test your patience with that. Its good you didn't fail. Relax your mind, you are taking him away with you soonest. You shouldn't worry about anything he does here. Once he boards the flight with you, he's all yours, my sister', she laughs with gusto.

A dry smile adorns Meghan's lips. She feels a burden off her mind as she tries to mull over the verity of her persuasion. After all, she chooses to admit her second idea. He is truly going to be hers soon once he boards the flight. Those scoundrels will not lay their claws on him anymore. She smiles once again, recuperates the hope to move on. If Mercy says it's okay, then its surely okay. She's always been there, has been their intermediary.

'Remember what happened between you and Raymond? Then, Tim and Andy and Jimmy and-?'

'Oh sis-, you know them all. It's okay, I don't wanna think about those rapscallions. I regret knowing them, not my past, you know?'

'I know but you gotta to be careful. I don't wanna count the number of men you've been with but your years in marriage. If you don't settle with one and learn to trust him, that will happen again. He will also become your rapscallion. This guy is your opportunity. You got him by chance. And if I were you, I will fight for what is mine and never give up'.

She walks to her bed, sits and begins to shift uneasily. What she says makes a lot sense. She always makes a lot of sense. However, something is more important.

'But- should I be stultified because I –',

'Just forget about that and make sure you visit tomorrow so I can show you how to forget about the gutter girl that answered the call. This is not an issue we discuss over the phone. Find time to see me tomorrow. And remember, come alone'.

'O-kay. I will see you first thing tomorrow morning', she slurs, feeling a little sleepy. She has had a long day.

'Alright, I will be expecting you. Goodnight'.

She drops the phone right next to her then begins to toss from side to side like a cat on hot bricks, pondering on Mercy's advice. She is seventy percent right on her judgement. It is factual she must trust him to end up in a trying marriage. It's not what she wants, and she can't muddle through a bad affair. For the next one hour, she laments about the sobering thought that he is one of the best ladies' man. This sends her whole being on fire. There should be only one man for a woman, she supposed. Besides, she wouldn't share her love with anyone. He's hers and only hers forever. As nature would have it, she falls into an untimely sleep.

4

A T FIVE MINUTES PAST six on Monday morning, Labi glides past a tawny-brown designer's pair of slacks. She heaves up to her waistline, looking down its close-fitting end erratically. Taking a leisurely stride to a framed floor mirror erected next to an old-fashioned wardrobe, she smoothens out the crinkles in a matching yellow short-sleeved shirt. In style, the shirt is tucked in slacks to reveal her curvaceous hips. Then a multihued choker put the last touch on her appearance. She is voguish, can't deny her devotion. Her true depiction manifests an inch away from a stunning stance. Her beauty remains, the curves and shapes still in place. What rules out the beauty queen? She has it all: a delicately modelled face, majestic physique, brown skin, and nice carriage. She simply evokes an aura of precision. She pulls a long breath then withdraws from the mirror downhearted.

What is the need? Of what need is it if my beauty isn't appealing to the man I live for? Neither beauty nor morals will change his mind. He will not forget his glorious trip because of me. Nothing I do will distract him from his plans to abandon me. He has shown to me, beyond doubt, that wealth surpasses everything in the world.

She breaks away from the mirror and saunters to his bed dolefully. She rolls up, cushions her head with a bent arm, the other tapping her belly, eyes surveying the wall. Her mind hovers to a preceding argument with him, then to counsels from friends and family and back to their last dialogue. Ultimately, all privileged advises surpass her attention. Everything seems apparent at present. Questioning her compulsion in the relationship, at the time, was deemed an acute unrestrained envy amongst her peers. She understands she worships him far too much, submits her all in the affair. As her loyalty travels far and wide, so speculations follows her. A mere look at him turns friends off. To them he doesn't appear genuine, no assured prospect with a man like him. What happens if he eventually betrays her? However, she was heedless of all visible gossips until now. How will she look at people straight in the eyes and apologize for looking through their inevitable guidance. In recent time, certain changes are evident. No more hand-in-hand walk around the campus or eye-catching cruises in the city. And when someone asks about this and that, she feels queasy, senses her gut in her head. It's weird the only place she gets a deserving solace is the depth of his wobbly arms.

Now, she is already suffering the indignity, doesn't have the gumption to antagonize no one any longer. She rolls her eyeballs, swears not to let it slip. That her one and only Dayo has been in an earnest affair with someone for five years and half and they are about to join in matrimony is a sheer dishonor. She sighs and rises to her feet.

She becomes aggravated in the room. What is more? Now, she is under the impression that Dayo has always put her under the shade. He goes about gratifying his desire without respect for her. Will she say that he's still the same man she knew? Never. He has metamorphosed into the shadow of himself. It hasn't happened before, since they met, that he will leave her alone in his apartment. He didn't return home to sleep, didn't go out with his phone. She claps her hands and grabs the phone again.

She examines his call logs then the inbox for new messages. *Sickening, sickening- oh my God! How will I survive this? How will I survive this?* She drops the phone. Her hands dash to her rescue. They clutch her pulsating head feelingly. It isn't enough, she drops to the bed. She believes, without doubt, that her beloved is queer in the head. There's absolutely nothing more to hide. In his absence, she ransacked every nook and cranny and discovered his travel document, copies of all his required documentation at the embassy. From her research, she discovered that Meghan was married three times before, and engaged several times. They have been together for five years and months now, even though he is still devoted to her, all pictures and old chats used for documentation attest to this. Meghan Connor, a fifty-eight year old insurer, is a Nigerian African- American, thirty years older than him. *This woman is set to destroy me. Why me? Why can't she leave my man for me?* There are proofs that she's been sending money to him, has been to Africa gazillion times to be with him. She pulls out her phone to track their recent dates. First, on the 26th of July 2010, coincidentally her birthday, he lied he was travelling with his father to see his ill uncle in their village. On his visit, he revealed he had a pool accident leading to disallowed calls in a hospital he was admitted. For that alone, he stayed away for three months without communication, palpably reveled in her presence in Africa. She shook her head at this, stamps her feet for always being his fool.

Second, on the 5th of February 2011, when he staged a false ground for his absence for three whole months, he got hired in a company in Ivory Coast. This also matches the date of her last visit when they had a secret engagement in his home town. There are photos of him and his folks, celebrating. She bit her finger at this. *Does it mean I'm so stupid to fall for all his lies at all times? Is there something I should have done to stop this from happening?*

Her heart jolts when Dayo himself pushes the door open and enters the apartment, sweating. His skin weathered black, face glistens and depicts the aftereffect of moisturizers in a brutal sunburn. The bus station was congested in the early hour, as usual. Over sixty-six passengers awaiting the same transit of just thirty-two commuters heading towards the same terminus. He is accustomed to it, must wait for another two hours before he would luck into his street. But for his phone, he is disconcerted. Besides, he forgot to lock his door before taking his leave. On second thought, he embarked on a long trek of about fifty-five minutes, escorted by nervousness in an inhospitable atmosphere.

'Labi, are you here? I mean, have you been here?', he inquires, leaves his door opened eagerly then dashes into the room. He detests her odd unsettling visits, mainly to keep a close watch on him. If that was right before, it isn't right now. No more obsession as he fights for his foreseeable future. His face twists when he peers around for his phone. His inner thoughts tell him there is no more secret, she has seen it all from the expression on her face. This time, he doesn't care if she leaves. He raises the mattress with no effort, slams it down then shoves books around on the desk. Four lockers fling forward in just six seconds, yet not in view.

Almost stepping on her feet, he walked past her to dive in his pockets. She is mesmerized, her wondrous eyes only following every direction he takes. He pays no attention to her, this hurts more. *Am I now an unwanted guest in his home? Does he think he is smart enough to use and dispose of me like this?* She sizes him up, prepares to answer his mindless question.

'By the way, what is wrong with me being here now? I have always been here before? Did you forget so soon? So, what is the problem now? I don't understand you', she steps away from a persistent hand near the pillow. He doesn't have her time and won't mind if she walks out of his glowing life. What matters is the phone. He clapped his eyes on his documents already.

'Where is my phone', he turns to her fiercely, his eyes burning with rage, his mind tied up with what she has done to wreck his hope. He has no private lock on it at Meghan's insistence.

'What intrigues you about coming here? Is this my first time here?'

'Don't you have lectures in school today? I mean- don't you have anything to do?', he brushes through her, looks under the mattress again. A gust of negligence engulfs her. She is an aggressor of their defensive privacy.

'How is that your problem? Did you ever worry about that? Why now? What is wrong with you?' Knowing what he searches high and low for, she chooses to disdain his effort. She knows what is about to happen, must find a way to prevent it. Her eyes survey the surrounding for her last chores before calling it a day. She grabs a broom slouching against the wall and begins to sweep. He gets more infuriated. The earlier she takes her leave, the better for him. He has only three hours to prepare for Meghan to pick him up at three.

'You see? You didn't close the door. You just barged in to ask me lot of meaningless questions. What's wrong with you?', she grumbles, sweeping. He bears her disruptions till the broom grazes and tweaks his hurting feet. He flares up.

'Please- you have to leave that work for me and go straight to your school right now. I don't like the idea of keeping you here during school hours. What do you want your mother to say about me? I will sweep my room myself; I'm also going out now', he collects the broom from her.

'School hours uhn? School hours that you never thought about since I've been coming here. O- kay I understand. I have to go- I have to give her a chance to visit. The queen of your heart is coming, right? Dayo- you are extremely stupid. So stupid to the core'. She collects the broom back, throws it on his desk. There, he caught his phone lounging and gazing at him, tired of all intrusive touches. He scurries to it and she grows more dejected.

'Oh- I see why I have to leave. I have seen every skeleton you hide in your cupboard, right? congratulations', she forces a threatening smile: a grin symbolizing his sadly ever after. At that point, she is determined to let go, no matter what. And now that he knows that she knows, what next? She folds her arms and watches him from behind.

Her combative instinct emerges, infuses a virulent force to strike while her saintly mind supersedes with formidable self-esteem and good nature. She stands still watching and stamping a foot grievously.

Not paying attention to her, he glances through his call log. Twenty-five missed calls from Meghan, three missed calls from his mother, two received calls from his sister, three received calls from Meghan. He is enraged. He hates to discover that she is about to reduce his optimism to rubble.

'Listen to me Labi, your obstinacy is so upsetting. I mean- this is not your phone and you are not allowed to answer my calls or reply my messages. That is so unwise. My phone represents me, and you have no business there'. He jumps down her throat, points the phone at her face. She takes three slow steps backward, cringes away from him, still wearing the sadistic smile. She must prepare for a strange turn of events, since he doesn't want her around him anymore. He now looks quite violent. *Is he about to hit me and send me away?* Only two weeks ago, her friend got beaten up and thrown in the street by an abusive boyfriend, to end a challenging relationship. She doesn't want to be a victim, will not allow that to happen. She looks down at his tautened fists and takes another step backward, shaking her head in surprise. One look at him shows he is truly done with her. He doesn't care to end it all in catastrophe. She has to be incredibly careful. Be that as it may, she isn't ready to give up. If they have to settle or part way on this day, she must know her fate in the relationship. There's nothing hidden anymore, the truth is revealed. An unflagging thought of betrayal rages her mind when she looks straight at him.

'First, let me remind you of something here, you touch my phone too, how is that a problem now? Have you been hypnotized to forget about you and I?' she demands calmly.

'Well, everything has changed. It is a huge problem if you don't keep your hands to yourself. I deserve my privacy for crying out loud. There is no you and I without marriage. I am not your husband!', he raises his voice. She takes another step forward, her feeble mind gloating on her next reaction.

'You know what? Tell me to go. Just tell me it is the end. Then, you also have to- break that vow now', she struggles to defeat the film of tears in her eyes. Her view turns hazy, a pang of guilt echoes from within. She believes she has bitten more than she can chew however what the future holds for them is dreadful.

'What vow? There wasn't a vow but child's play. Please spare me!'.

'What?!'

His phone begins to ring. He looks down at it and kicks the air. Meghan honey surfaces on the screen. Labi breaks down and begins to cry.

Oh my God! What have I gotten myself into? How am I going to cope with this trouble? If she can just leave and let me be, I'll be happy. What more is there to hide? She has seen it all, has even engaged in a conversation with her. Fine, that's it. And there's nothing new under the sun.

He goes around her in a jiffy, grabs his shoes and leaves her alone in the room. She cries out louder, screams like a baby and gives in to defeat. She feels her emotional trauma rolling her from edge to edge of the room but doesn't care about anything except the love she savored for years.

Her deep affection hysterically pushes her on the verge of trickery- an unpreventable misfortune that no human can resolve. In the midst of her trouble, she predicts the consequence of his action even though he feels nothing for her again.

For Dayo, life goes on. He decides on a path much more profitable and purposeful than a mere love affair in the bosom of poverty. Money is the key to every good thing in life. To make it quick, he chooses to cross the stream where it is shallowest. He wants to be called reputable names, associate with celebrities and live a lavish life of the rich and distinguished men in the society. *What is the essence of a love affair that brings nothing but lust for morals?* That is an old-fashioned reward for a genuine but futile passion. What trends in the contemporary age is love for riches. *Yes, marry your way out of poverty!* In his family, he wishes to commence the generation of men raising kids abroad and sending huge sum back home for assets. If fate has it that they will still be married in the future, then thank God for her lucky star.

'Hello, Meghan. I'm so sorry I didn't take your call last night. I left my phone charging in my neighbor's apartment'. He thinks the lie should work since there is always power outage everywhere.

'Oh- seriously? Who was the lady that answered your call? She was so rude and mean. She-'

'Never mind. I told you lot of girls are so disturbing right here. That was my neighbor's daughter, she's been so insistent. And I was with Segun last night. I tried calling you with his phone, but it was off the entire night'.

She sighs into the mouthpiece. Pauses for a moment and says, 'I was mad at you. I turned off my phone'.

'Mad at me for nothing? Come on, you can call my friend or his wife. I slept in their apartment. I told you about that before I left your apartment yesterday. That crazy girl wanted to frustrate you'.

'Me? Never-', she sighs again. Did she believe him? She tries to marry her faith to the lies. If he was lying and not being sincere to her, Mercy's advice sets him free. When there's a will, there will always be a way.

'When do you want me to pick you up? We need to talk'.

With that, he breathes an air of relief. He makes up his mind to walk elsewhere and avoid the obstacle in his room: to prevent an evil trying to bedevil his luck.

'You know what? Pick me up in Segun's apartment. I want him to see you before we travel. He said a lot about you last night'.

'Really? Uh- okay. Be there in two hours, is that okay? I'm with my sister right now'.

'That's fine. See you. I love you'.

'Love you more. Kisses'.

The phone rings off. He begins his journey to Segun's house, acclaiming a favorable chance to express his love. In her company, nothing seems achievable. Readily, he prepares to block her with his friend, so she won't find him in his apartment again. *What sort of trouble is this? What have I put myself into? I need no serious relationship in my life right now. In my youthfulness, I can't be unfortunately hooked down by poverty. Never! It has to be money first and love follows.*

He hastened up his steps, looking straight at the same bus station he avoided when he headed home earlier.

Unfortunately, he trekked back there to join the next bus. *All that will soon be over.* The time has arrived to begin a new life- a life free from routinely suffering. His life is in his hands if he can take charge and resist his problems. In as much as he knows how much Labi has supported their relationship, he is ready to make it up to her. He will, indeed, not just walk away without appreciation or compensation. First, he will excel, and every other thing comes next.

5

'YOU CAN'T CHANGE YOUR mind -just because of that. Once he gets on that flight with you, he becomes your slave'. Mercy gives Meghan a knowing look, unveiling denied truths about her love life. Where is her womanly wile to perform magic, make those men dance to her tune? She doubts if she has one. What baffles her mostly is her free acquaintance with footloose and fancy-free lovers, tastefully ensnaring her wallet. Once a mission is accomplished, she is left in a pathetic mood like a dying duck in thunderstorm. She never learnt from her unaffected bloopers or tried swaying them to restructure her life. Being siblings doesn't make them the same. There is a clear-cut divergence between them: with her considerable exposure, gallantry and firmness. On a whim, she was about to let go again. Never. As long as she toils for love within her field, she is willing to help on this one.

'Mercy. In our last conversation, you said all men are the same but- your hubby isn't like that, is he?', in her curiosity, she widens her eyes, cocks her braided hair aside, her hoop ear rings dangling in the same direction. Dayo is the first African and the most admirable in her life. Unlike her exes she knows so well in their habits, culture and outlook,

Dayo is different. But what makes him more refined than her brother-in- law?

'You mean my darling husband? He is so loving and adorable', privately, she intends to gloss over the matter. It's a lot more than she envisioned; a journey bumpier than it appears. She met him in the University, many years ago, in the same Faculty of Arts but different departments. There was a year dating followed by a quick proposal and nuptials in a Pentecostal church. Making a choice in an environment she was nurtured into adulthood makes life easier for her. They've had a lot of unresolved issues swept under the carpet, but her maturity is also a plus to prevail over difficult times. Only two months after their holy union, he changed. He would stay away from home for days, in warm cuddles of veiled followers, lavishing family resources and telling elephant lies. His obsession for younger girls aggravated her condition every day. The older Mercy gets, the more aversion and haven for dispassion she gets. She better be young than suffer negligence. He lost interest in her and their love crumbled progressively.

'Meghan- to secure a good man in a marriage isn't easy. I fiercely fought to have him forever'. She summons up all she has been through with him in just a short time and shakes her head in sheer empathy for the generation of women.

'What? Forever? You don't know the future- cannot tell if he will change tomorrow. And- what do you mean fierce? Do you get in a fight with everyone to win him over? That's not cool- it can cost you dearly. For instance, a jail term, you know?' She rolls her eyeballs doubtfully. Mercy grabs a knife form the kitchen, smiling, confident in her transgression. She places a peeled large onion on a chopping board and dices it smartly. Its past one, almost lunch time for her family. She has to prepare a rosy jollof rice for her kids before they return in their school bus within an hour. There is no justification for shambling around the house without preparing their meals. Meghan washes a pot for her, set the burner to fry the vegetables. As long as she hangs around, she must lend a hand. Again, Mercy breaks into a sullen smile, thinking about her question and the best answer to provide.

'Fighting is a crime, you know? And I don't have the power to lie in wait for women like me- for his sake. You need to understand the fact that I can't bushwhack anybody for him'. She watches the pot heat up; tiny simmering bubbles take shape in corners. A stream of oil sloshes down a large bottle and regulates the heat. It's way too much for her cooking. Mercy reaches for the pot and pours out some oil, still smiling.

'You better learn to cook this. You are about to marry a man from here. And they enjoy jollof rice and chicken so much', she turns down the heat. She smiles along, withdrawing from the spot. It's time to learn.

'You are not going to fight anybody. You fiercely use your discretion to keep him forever'.

'How?'

'I'll explain- but first you have to understand something. There's ninety nine percent likelihood of a man having extramarital affair than his wife. Do you agree with me?'

'Sure'.

'That's the reason you put in that effort'.

'How?' Her question hasn't been answered desirably. She asked how, not why.

'Dave used to rob Peter to pay Paul'. She makes a loud sound with the board, sniffs and blinks off some prickly vapors.

'How do you mean? Make that clear', she sniffs too. Her eyes were beginning to hurt. She hates slicing onions but loves its great taste in African delicacies.

'Money cannot buy love. You can't use your money to win his heart completely. I mean- it's just a matter of time. He will rob Peter to pay his Paul in the end'. She resumes her work to keep pace with the time she has spent talking. In seconds, the vegetables slide from the board into a smoking oil, shrieking with jubilance. A familiar aroma fills the air.

'Mercy- you are getting more and more confusing. Hit the nail on the head. What do you mean-rob Peter to pay Paul and how do you fiercely make him yours forever?'

'Yes-this is it. If you buy him over with your money as you are about to do now, he will take that money from you and use it to pin his true love down. That explains rob Peter to pay Paul', she smiles down at the pot, stirs on, relieves trapped onion and pepper.

This doesn't go down well with Meghan. Anger, fear and frustration visit her face. Her heart sinks as she gets it clear. She is the one trying to buy a man over with money while her sister is an example of a lady being cherished with dishonest money from love. *Impossible, incredible.* Now it dawns on her that it's not about the region. There are good and bad people anywhere in the world. From her statement, she learns that love is natural, you can't buy love with money. However, as it is right now, what is her fate if she gets nothing back from Dayo?

'Meghan, let's call a spade a spade. This guy may not have natural love for you. He may love someone else and just-'

'Oh- please, Mercy, you know what? Now, I don't understand you. I just do not understand you. This moment you are positive, next moment, you are negative. What is my fate? What do you advise me to do?' she shifts tautly on the sofa, rises from the seat and begins to pace around the room. Mercy seasons her cooking, adds up some water, then pours in some parboiled rice in a jiffy. She mustn't waste the whole time talking and at the same, must come to a conclusion before the kids arrive. No mention of adult's subjects in their presence.

'Come on, Meghan, I won't let that happen to you. Sit down and learn from your sis. I'm always here to help', she beams at her, drags her back to her seat, 'now, be attentive. What is worth doing is worth doing well. If you genuinely love him, then we can make him stay forever. I'll teach you what I did to make Dave stay forever'.

'What if I did nothing, would he have left me?'

'Sure. He will- after robbing you to pay his Paul. Smart up-girl!'

'Humph- I'm all ears'. She shudders, gets impatient. That he essentially intends to make the most of his privilege, saddens her. She is quite disappointed in him.

Mercy ultimately lets the cat out of the bag. She has ended her narration and Meghan is still flabbergasted. Did she do the whole of that to have him forever? Was it that tough? Why did she go that far? Her eyes fly to a wooden casing sheltering his recent picture. In the subconscious, she begins to feel sorry for his dominated life: a life curbed underneath her resolute feet. He is a pencil in her hands as he gets influenced to put her first in all matters. *And that is what he deserves to be! A controlled idiotic robot for robbing Peter to pay Paul.* It isn't long when the pity diminishes. He played too smart and she outruns him. Now, it's all about her. Is she ready to do the same to him and have him forever?

'You know what, Mercy? I need to think about this. I can't just take that kind of decision. That's a bit scary. You are so unbelievable', she smiles with a corner of her mouth.

'Your phone is ringing'.

'Oh- I didn't hear that', she pulls it out from her bag. It's time to drive fifteen miles to a location she picks Dayo up. She puckers her brow.

'What's up?'

'It's time to pick him up for our date. We are also hanging out with his friends today. I have to go', she looks straight in her eyes, afraid of her confession. Out of the blue, she begins to feel unsafe around her. Her countenance unravels a true change of mood and she leans over to assure her. The phone begins to ring again.

'Answer him. He won't stop until he robs you to pay his Paul- but trust me, I'm here for you', she reiterates, touching her chest. She is desperate nonetheless; she may think through her method in the future. Who knows?

'Hello- honey, how are you?', she meets her sisters gaze, sees a pugnacious look. Is that jealousy or hatred? In any case, she isn't ready to judge anyone until their affair hits the rock. She is not of those thoughtless people easily coaxed into a sinful conviction. She needs time to mull over it.

'Alright, be there in thirty minutes. There shouldn't be traffic on the way right now'. She rises to leave; her sister walks her to the door. To all intents and purposes, she has done all she can to evade cold arms of deception and betrayal. Now, the ball is at her feet at this critical moment: she chooses to keep him or let go of him after she glories in her attainment. A horse is forced to the stream but never driven to drink. She is not obliged to follow every advice she gives.

'I will get in touch with you-no- I'm gonna call you tomorrow. Today, I'll be so busy. Okay-bye sis-have a good one', she embraces her.

'I will call you too. Remember all I told you. Be smart enough to keep what is yours. Yours forever, you know?' she adjusts her top for her, smiling. The smile vanishes, and she looks serious.

'Mine forever. Yes- you are right. Thank you, sister. I appreciate. I have to go'. She smiles to the door.

Mercy stands gazing at her delicacy: all rosy and yummy. Food is ready and school bus arrives in five minutes. Her hubby also arrives in two hours, no extra time spent outside work except it's necessary. It's like that, has been like that and will always be the same till death parts them. Come rain or shine, he stays there for her and her children. She admits, within herself, that its worth her time and effort. It's worth forever. As for her sister, she understands she doesn't comprehend the culture, doesn't know the way it works. Whatever happens in the end is her choice. We all have choices to make in life: good or bad.

6

IT'S A HOT NOON. The sun is up and doing, wafting its cruelty on vulnerable pedestrians. Busy eyes lead on a lonesome and grubby road, and back in quest of deficient shields stripped by hostile atmosphere. Only in ten minutes interval, occupied buses drive past briskly. Despairing and weary commuters make haste, beckon for consideration, then turn away in sheer dissatisfaction. It's a pretty long walk to the bus station where automobiles queue up accordingly, by terminal. Standing by the road takes forever, the station is easier. The thought of sunburn keeps everyone positioned at the spot, with optimism to possibly get a vacant bus, if there's ever one. And getting one doesn't establish leaving the spot in the face of geared-up tussle. Altogether, twenty passengers battle for only three spaces in a bus. It is, indeed, survival of the fittest as they sneak a look at one another, make a clean sweep of their trailing sweat intermittently.

Labi shades her luminous face with her left hand, leans the other on her waist, also anticipating leaving the curb. She feels a rivulet of perspiration coursing through her backside and another one meandering from her chest down her belly. She grimaces at her dislike for sweating. It makes her sick and uneasy. What she desires now is crowding through the road, pull off her outfit, and take a cool shower to ease the radiating heat. While her wish predominates over shrouding essential parts of her body, so the society supports dressing to the teeth to foster virtuous females. *Oh God.* Even though its hot as blazes, at no point should she lose this communal sense of values. Be that as it may, she endures and smiles halfheartedly.

In next to no time, she turns to meet the steady gaze of a good looking, averagely tall young man, standing just too close for comfort. She was overly engrossed in her enthusiasm; she didn't observe him for a while. He holds his gaze. She takes a step rearward and he breaks into an unnoticed heroic smile, progressing in fine style.

'Hello beauty', he murmurs, beneath a deep voice.

'Yes? Can I help you?', she gives a respectable distance. It's a period of year when girls are abducted for rituals, servitude and trafficking. In recent news, there are accounts of discovered corpses but missing vital parts. Steering away from strangers decreases the risk of being a target for hired slayers in the urban areas. Again, she takes another step. He comprehends why and upholds the gap between them.

'What can I do for you?', she snaps but he still doesn't care. A bus arrives at the time and there is a scuffle. As five commuters make it, she gets so infuriated for being distracted by him. She returns a face like thunder.

'You look familiar- so familiar. Have I met you somewhere before?' he touches his temple ambling down memory lane. She has no time for this.

'It can't be me. I don't know you and I haven't met you anywhere before. And I won't ever in my life-meet you anywhere'. She reckons, plunging her gawp through his dusty and old-fashioned shoes. She focuses on the road, watches another bus approaching. Her nicely manicured fingers pave the way for a feat, wave magnificently at the vehicle. He admires her from head to toe, thinking of how to rivet her attention, since his first trick didn't carry his plan into effect. She seems not easily charmed by his superficial child's- play.

'Can I meet you- please? I like you a lot and I want to know you. What is the beautiful name, please?', he says passionately but too repulsive for her. She clears her throat and spits next to her. He isn't turned off. He admires her height, face and posture whilst she gets too uncomfortable around him. Will she be stupid to disclose her name to a hateful stranger? She shot him a bad stare, watching the next bus disappear with another two commuters. Her eyes follow them avidly. Perhaps, his distraction causes more delay in the sun. If he has no car to chauffeur her off the sun or a bargain to enhance her deteriorating life, then what is his need? What is the need for a man that offers nothing but uses and dump her like garbage in a bin? *Just like the case of Dayo. They appear as nightly thieves, rob her of her possession and even rub it in.* At the same time he chances another attempt, the reflection of her past treacheries come into play. She gloats over her mistreatment and takes it out on the young man.

'Can you please spare me? What do you take me for? A prostitute?', she walks away from him and joins a group of passengers gathering a stone's throw away from them. He stands transfixed at the spot, astonished at what his blind impulse blossomed into. He begins to regret advancing on her when four other people turn to laugh at him. He remains where he is, pretending nothing happened. It's the surest way he can manage the situation. Labi looks away from him. Being a victim the second time is an impossibility she brings into reality.

In less than ten minutes after, a bus with twelve open seats arrives. Eighteen commuters stream down for space. No effort spared; all seats are taken. An old man of about eighty years tag along, begging for a position, searching from face to face for compassion. Wrathful commuters eye up his obnoxious appearance, wondering whose concern is it to fight for survival late in life. Most youths in the society detest the old, engaging in their contemporary uphill battle. There are often unanswered questions like: where was he at his early time? Or cant his children look after him? The blameless old clash with his societal misery, pull through futility towards an imperfect end. For his fragility, he watches his shackled willpower take a heavy toll on him. Unlike fifty years back when he was full of life, he can't help himself. He has, since, given over to age to rule his life style: feeding, walking, chewing and all things he imagines in his enervated head.

'Please, let- me- in', he pleads weakly, his veined oscillating eyes, drifting here and there.

'Where? On top of the vehicle? Do you not see that all spaces are occupied? Please step back before I lose my temper!', the bus operator howls him away. As a tradition, he just had a sip of a locally prepared gin and is under its influence. He sees fire on a pitiless impostor, not an old defenseless man. From the back seat, Labi gets too worried about him. She puts two and two together and makes to vacate her seat for him.

'No-don't dare touch that man. Let him in', she screams at him, half rising from her seat.

'Where is his space in this bus? Do you want him to sit on your laps? Sit down and be quiet!'. He throws his hand in the air going berserk. She understands his plight, liquor is in control. It makes him overly irrepressible the whole time and no one worries about his self- destruction or the danger he poses to vulnerable customers at his mercy. What matters is getting away from the atrocious sun and reaching a relaxing destination on time. She won't be in war of words with him, not even their seemingly right-thinking driver, who looks straight at the ready and waiting road seriously. He can't wait to turn on the ignition and maximize his time.

'I will alight for him. Excuse me- let him take my space', she rises from her seat, alights from the vehicle.

'You will? Will you? Are you a Mother Christmas? Go ahead, don't waste our time here'. They give her a chance to leave. Slowly, kindly, she returns to her previous condition. It isn't over till it's over. The old man climbs into her space in slow progression, tiredly. A number of heads bend to avert an imaginary stench. Labi is admired by only a few for her show of respect or patience to step out. The old one cannot thank her enough for making him escape pepper upon injury. After he faced disappointment from a fraudulent son, who promised him heaven on earth but failed, he had to walk there empty handed. He stood in the sun for approximately two hours for the want of transport and money. Looking straight at Labi, he begins to pray for her.

'My daughter may the good lord grant you a happy life and a good marriage'.

'Amen, go on. I have paid for the fare. You don't have to pay him anything. And use this to buy something for yourself', she tucks a note in his shaky hand. He peers down at it, looks back at her face. He is wordless. He nods and prays on.

'Enough of your drama. Mission accomplished. At least, with that, you can stay in your house for a while. Do us that favor, okay?', the bus driver shouts from the front. It dawns on the commuters that both bus operators are birds of the same feather. They are visited by panic.

Labi hurries back to the same spot, trudging through the crowd to face the same exasperating process. She reflect, a little, on the old man's prayer, then about Dayo and his journey. *Marriage? Marriage my foot! Surely, he has no idea.* With a heavy heart, she blinks back the warmth of the sun, having precognition of a dreadful mental image. She pictures her beloved loving an unknown woman and having a happy life ever after. She sighs. She wishes she could turn back the hands of time or increase the number of years he has to stay. She is a weak kitten watching him slip off her fingertips.

'Young lady- are you going or not? Do you enjoy the sun?', a middle-aged man breaks into her thought. Four different buses have arrived after she joined the crowd, yet she stood and stared vaguely. She appeared not to be in a hurry at all. When her mind travels back from the realm of imagination, she peers around and notices there are only two of them left.

'Thank you, sir', she hurries into the bus too, her diligent eyes wandering through a chatty circle to study a new environment, the driver and the vehicle itself. Unlike the first one, everything is different: nice interior, relaxing seats, neat metals and most importantly, a safer driver. The journey begins at precisely 5pm.

They proceed on a crude, bumpy road: chasm, standing water, splashes, switch and swerve alongside slapdash maneuvering. The driver doesn't occur like himself; he is a ravening wolf in sheep's covering, a foe behind the wheels. With chin turned up and face twisted, he tosses his nervous travelers into unpredicted potholes, climbs and descends obtrusive bumps. He hears all lamentations and entreaties from behind, reaches for his radio and turns up the volume to supersede disruption. He is accustomed to their habits, so he turns a deaf ear to them. He cares only about delivering them to their terminal and starting a new journey back to where he began. It's a cycle he must complete up to eight times before dusk to make ends meet. It's a routine on a route to provide for the bus fees. Sometimes, life gets terribly challenging and he gets tired of doing the same boring job every day.

He tries swerving to escape a pothole but misses. The bus plunges, burst out with a loud rustling noise then zooms off, in rapid succession. Passengers surge forward and grip anything within reach for safety. Heads tilt backwards, bottom shifts sideward and almost gets displaced. Flashes of rage cross their faces as they bump along.

'Oh God, you just hit my head on the window. Take it

easy, we are not in a hurry!', a man in the front row yells behind the driver. He rubs his forehead and looks down at his palm to check for blood. Fortunately, he isn't bleeding, only has a protuberance he expects to ripen before arrival.

'Oh my God, what kind of bus is this? Is this a suicide mission?', he adds, still rubbing his head. The driver utters no word. He turns around to catch a glimpse of his anguished face, then returns his face to the road. He unavoidably enters another pothole, climbs up a bump and speeds on. Sad eyes shoot him malicious stares from behind. He doesn't care about their lives and well-being as the money he makes off them.

'Take it easy man. Don't bury us in the potholes', another man cautions. He lowers his gaze, spectates him in his rear mirror and ignores him too. He chooses to be silent to keep his work going. Silence accomplishes his mission on daily basis. The only time he talks is when he is not driving. No one will provoke him to talk, no matter what.

Labi keeps mute, just like most of the travelers. From time to time, she merely turns and stares when people talk and yell around her. She blinks behind a pair of dark glasses, deeply engrossed with the thought of her life. Whenever she hears a protest, her mind is suspended. All the inevitable societal issues surrounding her are quite disappointing. She rubs elbows with them whenever she is outside her home, can't get away from them. Has she ever noticed how disturbing they get or how much of it she suffers in a day? Never, only in recent times when she is about to lose her beloved, partly due to the same societal woes. She thinks he has a good reason to get away from the eyesore plaguing him. For him, it is over, yet life is not the same forever. No one to make her flight of fancy come true, no beloved to fill her heart with joy. For once, since she is braced to accept the problem, she begins to see how patently painful it is to live through all of that every day. *Can't I leave too? I can find somewhere to go too.*

When the bus almost arrives at its station in twelve minutes, everyone is relaxed. No more potholes and craggy roads ahead. They breathe a sigh of relief and then occupy their minds with their undertakings- either good or bad. There is a pregnant lady in the second row. For a reason, she opens her bag and closes it again. On her third attempt, she makes up her mind to bring out whatever she is hiding. Before their eyes, she unwraps a large leaf of bean cakes. Its aroma fills the air. Noses sniff to locate the pleasant perception. Finally eyes nestle on them, mouths begin to water. They look so delicious and sumptuous. She is too hungry to discern a desirous gesture around her. It is her third trimester; she eats more to grow her baby.

'Oh- that looks really nice. Where did you get the akara from?', an old lady sitting just next to her inquires looking straight in her food. She swallows greedily, wishing they were hers. She hasn't eaten anything good that morning. People have been so unfeeling to her.

'There. Right there- where we began the journey. We were standing there for over an hour. Didn't you see her peddling?', she devours more balls, regretting why she answers her stupid question. Can't she get her reddish eyes off her food? It's annoying how people take their gluttony with them everywhere, even in the public.

'I never knew it was this nice. Looks nice- really- really good', she smiles, still looking at the remnant hungrily.

From the corner of her eyes, she detests her. The earlier the bus arrives, the better for her. She needs a healthy space and refreshing air of privacy, away from the crooked looking face next to her. To her left sits a young man, looking away from the food. He looks lost in a deep thought, perchance spacing off till the journey ends, just like she imagines. If we were raised the same way, the world would be the best place to be. She darts a revolting look at the old one and continues eating. With that, she disregards her.

Man proposes, God proposes. Hastening and straying minds fill the bus, anticipating a scheduled arrival. No one predicted the end of the thirty minutes journey until the unexpected happened.

'Driver- driver park this bus. Stop the bus! Blood of Jesus. Holy ghost fire', someone screams from the back seat. Pandemonium broke out, the bus screeches around a neighboring curb like a bat out of hell. Emergency light is turned on before he hops down and slams the door.

All heads turn in the same direction.

'What happened? Is she in labor?', a man like a yard of pump water asks blankly. He looks from to face searches for a response, but no one answered. He hurries to a woman helping the victim and asks the same question.

'Leave me alone. Does your wife labor in the neck, if you have any-', she snaps at him, sizes him up. It isn't time to hurry anywhere. Now the bus is empty, and a sufferer is laid on the bare ground for safety. They do not know what to do to keep her alive. For those that have encountered child's labor, it doesn't occur with choking or gasping, the eyes do not protrude like she is about to give up. As she holds her neck and struggles for survival, there is an indication that she ate something that leads her between life and death. Afterall, she was seen wolfing lots of bean balls only a few minutes earlier.

'What sort of nonsense is this now? Can't we continue this journey anymore? What kind of delay is this?', the same old lady sitting next to her in the bus begins to complain. She gets so grumpy, paces around in a relaxed manner. She offers no assistance to the dying woman. With only one person observing, she begins to keep a distance, and farther- farther she gets till she walks away like greased lightning. Unfortunately, she wasn't the only one on a mission in the vehicle. He keeps his weather eye opened around her, especially after her hard-hearted utterances and gratuitous retreat from the group. He grows suspicious of her, while thinking of protecting the lady and her baby.

She is dying, now her eyes are dilating. She stretches on the ground and starts convulsing. For the sake of the guiltless child, he needs to react quick.

By the time he looks up again, he decides not to mind his mission as he wanted to. He must go after her. She walks so fast- as fast as her legs can carry her, the fag end of her scarf dancing in the air. He races after her.

'Excuse me, hold on – hold on for a moment', he says breathlessly, gasping for air.

'Yes? What is it? Why are you after me?', she sounds rather too aggressive before he says a word. He knows why he is there; no one needs to tell her.

'Please- forgive her. Set her free, she won't do that again', he says, still panting.

'Forgive who? For what? What are you talking about?

You must be crazy, very stupid. Get out of my way', she pushes him and continues going. She barely took the next step when he grabs her elbow. She knows him and they know themselves. They all have a mission and this time, she fails.

'Stop right there! You have a choice to release her now or I will hand you over to the crowd there. And you know what that means? Jungle justice. Set her free now. Come with me'. She leads her back to the scene with an unsmiling face. She has no choice but to let her off the hook. That's much more preferable to facing a public shame and being stoned to death as he said. Her eyes darken with anger as she approaches the scene. Many also suspect her already when he was spotted running after her. Who else could it be, if not her? She was the only akara seeker in the vehicle.

By now, the woman writhes in pain. Every first aid they comprehend has been administered on her despite their heightened fear of the police. You are accountable for your reports. And if a victim dies, you are also a victim. In spite of this rampant awareness, they summon up the courage to give a hand her, but she remains same as ever.

When the evil one stands next to her body, her situation gets worse than before. She begins to foam in her mouth, her pupils disappear slowly as convulsion sets in. Women begin to cry, men smolder with indignation.

Labi keeps her distance from the crowd. She watches the prey with eyes full of pity and prays for her survival. She has slim chances of persistence now as she foams in her mouth and widens her eyes like a bubble about to explode. The salivary content slobbers from her mouth, descends her jaw and streams down her round pleated neck to a drenched blouse. She feels disgusted and turns away from her irritably, sadly. At the same time, she hears clamor around her. Someone familiar, the same woman that sat next to the victim in the bus is being forced down to free her.

'I told you I will- if you let me', she promises the mob, entangling a rope she tied on her arm, underneath a traditional blouse, only by magic. Mystically, by means she can explain, she suspended the food in her throat when she refused to offer her, at least, a bite of her food. No medication will release her, except simple regulation of the rope. And that is the magic that gives her a breath of relieve.

The pregnant lady looks from face to face. She only recalls the time she fell from her seat and started choking. She didn't understand why she is being surrounded by all the people in the bus, including the driver. Did something happen to her? Was she unconscious? She looks down at her wet blouse masked by her own spittle, mucky body and of course, her large tummy.

She strives to stand on her feet- to end the shame she already admitted inadvertently. Bystanders pitch in and help her back on her feet. In the twinkling of an eye, the culprit and her attacker disappear. They aren't discernible anywhere, not even on the lonesome road.

'Where is the lady and the-?' curiosity drops in on them.

'I don't know anything. I don't know', a woman says raising her arms in great fear. She would rather not say a word than be a victim too. Obviously, they vanished into thin air. She knows the consequence of her impiety and doesn't want to get killed. Many have fallen in her traps; it just appeared to be a bad day.

'Have we been followed by evil? Can someone just explain what happened here?' a timid man inquires.

'You saw it happen. The woman is free, so let's get out of here before they return in multitude'. They all hurry back in the bus, the driver first. Tongues wag, curses follow, prayers supersede. One after the other, they are all seated. Two women help the casualty back to her position. No one takes the *akara* seeker's seat, only hers is left empty.

Labi is the last to get in the vehicle. Seeing her mum and returning to her hostel on the same day is impossible, after wasting the whole time on the way. Now, her mind is so full of mysterious thoughts about the verity of voodoo. *Is voodoo real? Wait a minute, did she use a charm to control the food in her throat? That was unbelievably gruesome. What will she gain from her sacrilegious feats? But for the man that came to her rescue, could she have passed away for eating in the public or on account of her supposed cupidity?* She claps her hands in disbelief. Her belief starts ringing true. She marries spiritually with her problem and imagines all probable impracticalities. In only two minutes, her endless journey ends by God's will. A little weight drops off her heart since the last time she was left by herself in Dayo's room. She smiles silently. What she just observed is somewhat the elucidation of her problems. She believes God made her witness that for a reason yet unexplored - a reason she is going to take full advantage of, come what may. *If voodoo is real as I observed with my eyes today, why can't I also take advantage? Does he think I'm going to give up just like that?*

Impossible. I'm never going to give up what is mine. I will fight strongly for what is mine. He is fiercely mine forever, he has no way out of my life, even though he tries. When there's a will, there's always a way. We must live in this country together.

7

DAYO LOOKS BROWNED OFF at a mention of Labi. In a last gasp effort to shun her and focus on his life, he took lots of debasing measures. He stops sleeping in his room and still blocked her number. There's nowhere they have been together that she will ever locate him again: she is barred from him everywhere. He wishes he never had to be hostile to her, wishes everything went on as proposed. When their relationship started off, there was no menace of parting until Meghan occurred in his life. He knows how much harm he has done to her, walking out on her, even if his accomplishment takes priority over all things right now. It's a deliberate dream lingering for realization from year to year. The time finally arrives to arise out of hardship and excel. He is determined not to die in a life of toil or allow this prospect slip through his fingers. Who fractures his ladder of victory to gratify a woman? Or methodically excuses his fortunes to earn a deserving honesty? *Who cares?* Mending his shortcomings saves her head from trouble too, so he doesn't regret his actions. In all sincerity, she has done ideally well so far, and loved him with all her human values, even though she hasn't money to take Meghan's place in his heart. He understands what she stomachs at the moment and is prepared to make it up to her before his departure in only two days. His conscience isn't dead, so he feels her burning emotion. Despite all his wrongs, should he still speak ill of her? No, he admits to not being a party to that. He pushes his food away, shifts his seat rearward, looking utterly dissatisfied.

'Honey- I am your wife- to- be. I want to know if there's any girl out there- you still have a love affair with. I don't want that to ruin our marriage. Tell me now, I need to know before we leave. I am your wife', Meghan pushes the food back to him like a boss ready to exert power.

'Do you want me to feed you?', she requests, holding the spoon, ready to lead the whole food down his throat.

'No', he rejoinders, sizing up a coarsely concocted jollof rice between his hands. If he grew up eating that mess all day, he would have died of constipation. From the corner of his eyes, he watches its overused oil flooding through the angles of a great mound, its lurid food coloring shimmering like a soiled anthill in the sun. Nothing about the food looks appealing except for her ordered grilled chicken wings, lying gullibly around its despicable counterpart. He grimaces, prays inwardly to elude her force of habit before he begins to lose concentration. She appears too bossy and extremely rude with the way she always wants to take charge of his resolution. If that's how she wishes to continue, he thinks they may not last longer. In no circumstances is he ready to relinquish his manly African power. He is a man still in control, always in control.

Without knowing, his unbeatable love for Labi surfaces. He imagines her vociferous tone lashing back at his intents, proving his self-seeking instinct wrong for going above and beyond. He closes his eyes against the distress, holds his head tiredly. He wishes he had the courage to tell her it is the end; tell her he chooses his luck over her, but he could not. The society is disobliging to cultivate or generate a worthy livelihood, not to mention talents. He recounts how many times he wandered in arduous search for a job after his graduation from the university. He moved from company to company with all commendable credentials, for at least, the lowest opening possible. He has no income, cannot make money without an occupation. But for his proper background, he would have resorted to crime. And even though he deems it fit to steal, the community has zero tolerance for robbery. He has watched thieves burnt alive and humans butchered in broad daylight for committing one crime or another. The police are not recognized or involved in jungle justice since a considerable mass of the population believe that every culprit suffers less pain in their custody. They want to see them cry, beg for existence and act as a precautionary measure for those who still nurse crime in their hysterical mind. He grows older each day and believes that, if care is not taken, he may watch and wait until he clocks fifty-two and still wander in squalor. As much as he loves her, he wants to sacrifice one precious thing for another.

'Are you okay? You look so unhappy today. Tell me, what is wrong?', she pulls his mind back to the food, smoking in his face. He takes a second look at it and lost his appetite.

'You. You make me sad', he looks straight in her eyes.
'How?'
'I told you I don't have an affair with anyone. I have just

you and no one else. Yet, you don't trust me. I am sad when you distrust me'. He shifts his chair further, wraps his arms across his chest. Now, his eyes rest upon her appearance. He thinks Labi or all his exes look better. Without a makeover, she is far too unattractive and is always a mismatch for him. It's like rivalling a torch with the sun. In spite of this, it doesn't matter. It is a means to an end.

'Calm down baby-calm down and let's talk it over', she pulls back a dining chair then sits adjacent to him, trying to appear sexier. She will do all things to win this handsome, hardworking and intelligent man but make every effort to pull him up and wind down the imperfections in his deceitful life. She knows he lies and must rectify that before they step up to marriage. At that point, she thinks of Mercy's strategy then says, 'someone answered your call and confessed she is your lover, what do you say about that? How can you explain that?'

Dayo sighs, then re explains to her. ' Listen to me Meghan. In this society, electricity is not stable. This is not America, okay? My phone battery was low, and I gave it –' he gives in to her disruption.

'To a neighbor to charge it for you. And she answered your call then claimed to be your love. How do you explain that?', she rants. Dayo gets irritated. If that is what he is going to deal with in the US, he is in trouble. He suspects trouble looking forward to his arrival. He can't escape it, no matter what. Sooner than he expects, she bangs the table just next to his food, extends a finger and warns vehemently, 'look, if you think you are smart, I am a lot smarter. Tell me if you have a relationship now- before we board that flight together or you will regret it there. You are not going to live in a country where you guys mess with your women. You will be in a lot of trouble. Trust me'.

She storms into the living room, fuming. This is only a tip of an iceberg but his jaw drops. He spectates the chicken wing suspend from the plate, away from a copious throw of rice around the table. His glass of water also spilled, splattered against the wall. He looks from the food to her face then back to the food. In his entire life, he hasn't been pressured by a lady. He believes in himself always. Her reaction already creates a detrimental inkling that he hasn't seen anything yet. There is more to uncover about this angel in his life.

He frowns at her threat, takes a second look at her. Is this the reason she has been alone? She sounds violent and aggressive. She doesn't seem like the beauty he knew before. In a short time, she has gathered the courage to intimidate him. Is this going to work for him? He rises up, pulls back his chair and made to leave. She comes around him and blocks the road.

'Where are you going? To your gutter girl? Heck nope. We have to talk it over now and listen- ', she pauses, reminiscing her sister's warnings about her past futile relationships before they decisively hit the rocks. She has to make it work whichever way, and stop acting up. Her first attempt to chance love in her home country must work out well. His mien already portrays unmingled despair within a short period. What if he decides to let go of all their endeavors together and walk away, back in the arms of the same lady they argue about? She will be a dead loss at investing if she expended that much and still has nothing to show off to her anticipative and well-meaning friends in

America. She sighs resignedly, then approaches him with forethought this time. She becomes so romantic.

'Honey- I'm so sorry. I love you so much- I really do and -I'm only scared. I don't want anyone snatching you from me. You are mine forever. I'm sorry if I annoyed you', she closes the door, opens his arms and wraps them around her, head stuck to his chest. He is astounded. He narrows his gaze, watching all her moves. Is she for real? He knows her mind and can tell she's being sincere. But she has no clue what his genuine objectives are. She has articulated her emotions innumerable times and its the reason she toured all the way there: thousands of miles away to search for love. What about him? Does he genuinely love her? The gospel truth is no. Their affair is only a means to an end, and nothing changes, no matter what she does. He doesn't care about whoever, doesn't need a love right now: not Labi or anyone. He understands she cares, and she won't let go, so his threat will always work.

'It's okay', he fakes a smile, walking back into the living room. She is pleased but not absolutely until he answers her worrying questions about the phone conversation. Not knowing what else to do, she clears the mess on the table, then disappears into the kitchen. Dayo takes a long breath, relaxes with a new plan. *I am being forced by circumstances to accept humiliating defeat from this lady. What was that about? She is so discourteous, haughty and charmless. What am I getting myself into? Is this going to work out for me after leaving my continent? What is she up to? Well, man proposes, God disposes. We shall see the end of the line.*

8

FROSTY DECEMBER APPEARS WITH a piercing climate. The season is dry, its penetrating wintry stream so severe. Anything dries up at this time: lips crack, skin flakes off and soles fissure like a fracturing earth. Body protective outerwear and moisturizers are also in great demand as commercial transaction of cold drinks declines drastically. Hospitals admit more cases of cold related illnesses, nearly every day. What is more to disguise? As trees are raided and rid of valuable defensive leaves and reliant birds, so masqueraded shower enthusiasts get uncovered with somewhat pallid manifestations across visible spots. The soil, in a fearless adventure, rebels with the rage of nature, encroach dwellings, smear houses. Necks squat down, arms retreat, and eyes dim in reverence for a zealous harmattan season.

Labi looks smart in a parti-colored sweat top over a blue skinny jean and low-heeled ankle boots. She emerges, on the double, in an urban street, leading to Segun's apartment, her neck sheathed in a light brown cashmere scarf. Earlier that day, she called Dayo's phone to her heart's content, yet unreachable. Her abortive tries strike her at the moment, didn't realize she has tried more than ninety-two times after the last moment he left her in his room. *What is going on? Am I dreaming? Has he left Africa?* For this belief alone, she has had wakeful nights. She has been to his room. It's under locks and keys. At that point, she is driven by her pessimism to explore every avenue to find him. She breaks into a quizzical smile as her mind unfolds the bitter truth she hates to admit. *Dayo has travelled out of the country. Unfortunately, I've been edged out of his life?* She becomes implausibly concerned about herself.

All for something, she watches her solitude eat away her physique, power, passion and pleasure. Nothing fascinates her like before, nothing occurs relevant in her life. In the beginning, their fathomable differences give only a rough time. She gradually learnt to come to terms with his new life and tough decisions. Now, it appears insoluble. And from the look of things, he is gone. His neighbor confirms that he hasn't been seen for the past one week. Did he relocate to another apartment? *He has travelled overseas, finally.* She grins, her mind busily centered on how to unearth the truth from his friend, if he knows anything.

Her quivering hand ascends an eventful wooden door, towards the bell. She narrows her view to read a tag printed in red and white, always there to welcome visitor. *With God, all things are possible*-she mumbles. Knowing how factual it is, she begins to pray for all possibilities in her life- all likelihoods that performs magic to erect Dayo in front of her and begin a new life. Who knows if he's hiding in the same apartment for a virtuous reason? If he turns up to open the door, then her difficulty is settled.

She is wrong. Soronje opens the door in a flash, squinting at her face to recollect where they have met earlier. They gathered twice in the same apartment before she also stopped seeing Dayo. Is she the one?

'Good morning. This is Labi, Dayo's fiancé. Do you remember me?', she fakes a broad smile, tries to keep her sorrow under wraps. A memory strikes her, and she recalls their last night out together at Severin lake, only three months ago. How could she forget her so soon? She runs her eyes over her in search of a transformation wonderingly.

'Oh- I'm so sorry. Come on in. It's quite a long time. Sorry the cold is too much- so much that you can barely straighten up. Where are you coming from this early morning, I mean, in harmattan season? It's so chilly out there. And why haven't we seen you in a long- long -time now?'.

Labi pauses, smiles on. Where will she start from, and what question will she answer first? She marvels at the wonder woman's inordinate talking tradition about her past and present and even the future she knows nothing about. She talks a mile a minute. If Segun is around, he will come to her rescue as the last time. But sadly, she seems not really in the mood today.

She merely follows her into their living room, still smiling and thinking about an entertaining discourse to begin. Her eyes fall on a soothing arm support and she grabs it. She sits in a sofa opposite her, feeling so nervous and uneasy.

'Why are you here this early?', she asks only one of her previous questions, also finding the coolest spot to sit. *Oh my God? Can she just go? I'm not here for her this morning. I don't want to talk and have head ache. Where is Segun or Dayo?*

'Actually', she pauses and clears her throat, searches for

the right answer to give. She mustn't know that she is there for Dayo- just for him.

'I stopped by to check on you guys'.

'Eh-eh, so kind of you, especially in this cold. Thank you so much. What happened to you? You look so lean, you look thinner than the last time I saw you. You know people get thin for different reasons-depression, exercise or whatever. You know? You look so different around your cheekbones', she hit the nail on the head, and she isn't happy about it.

'Oh- me? There's a difficult course I took in school. I had to study really hard to pass it last week and -it really affected me. School isn't ea-sy', she slurs the last word, wishes she shut her mouth.

'Oh- I'm sorry you said what?', she demands to hear the last word. Labi gets tired of her incessant approaches. She leans forward to repeat herself and possibly prepare to leave. She isn't comfortable around a numbskull.

'School is not easy, you know?'

'You are right. That's the reason I dropped out', she smiles from ear to ear and Labi rolls her eyeballs. Shouldn't that be a secret? She will be embarrassed to disclose that kind of secret to anyone.

She gathers herself together, exploring the apartment. Her attention drifts into an appointment she has at 10am, towards completing her final year project in school. She turns back to check the time on a big clock suspended from a wood- paneled wall. Its 7:45am. She needs to accomplish her mission without delay and take her leave to keep up with another scheduled exam at 9am.

'Is Segun around? I want to see him before I go', she requests in a jiffy.

'Alright, I'll call him for you right away', Soronje rises at a snail's pace and saunters in the direction of their bedroom, her protruding tummy in the lead, her left hand on her waist. Labi gapes till she is out of sight. Soronje is pregnant, obviously. She also looks different, though hers is a buoyant transformation she would have chosen over her present situation. *Oh God, Soronje is pregnant. She is the same woman Segun swore never to marry, now she carries his baby. Obviously, their relationship is getting more serious. What becomes of me if sincerely, Dayo is out of the country? It means all our years together is a complete waste. oh - I'm finished. Where will I start from? Oh gracious God.*

'Labi bay-by. Labi, the queen of beauty. How are you today?', Segun beams walking up to her. He is always so delighted to see her. God comprehends how ecstatic he feels in her presence, even though she isn't for him. For all he knows about her, she is a paradigm of beauty, intellect and morals. Sometimes, he thinks she is too good for Dayo's gambles and even desires her, in place of garrulous Soronje.

'Since you didn't find me, I decided to find you today', she rises from her seat, embraces him in a customary amicable manner. She pulls away, he holds on for seconds and asks, 'Labi, is everything okay? You look different', he examines her face pitifully, knowing all her worries. None other than Dayo.

'I – am-fine', she looks away bashfully.

He pats her back saying, 'don't worry. Everything will be alright, okay? Everything will be fine'. She nods, sinking back in the sofa. He takes the seat opposite her, angles his head, listening.

'Segun', she drops the arm rest, almost slipped off the sofa.

'Labi, calm down, okay? This is Segun with you. Just tell me what the problem is, and we shall resolve it together'. His smile fades away. Absently, he touches his jaw with a finger.

'It's about Dayo. I haven't seen him for the past six weeks now. I have been to his apartment and his neighbor told me that he doesn't live there anymore. There is even a new tenant there now. Could anything have happened to him?', she pulls back the tears in her eyes. Segun deciphers her standpoint and sighs heavily. Poor girl, suffering from unfeeling doom of love. What should he say to her? How will he divulge his heartrending certitude before he waved him goodbye, at the airport, alongside his new love? From the beginning he was there. He witnessed mostly aspects of their serious relationship in the past years. He was carried along with spasmodic arguments and resolutions. Almost all the time, he was invited to settle differences and even propose a future together. Why did he also attest to the end? And how is he going to tell her it is the end? He drops his head for a moment then glimpses at her steady and hopeful gaze. He has to spit it all out, express her providence in the abortive affair. It takes the edge off, prepares her to move on.

'Labi, Dayo is gone. He travelled out of Africa just ten days ago'. He let the cat out of the bag.

Shock waves scurry through her face, her heart jolting all along. Her ears are mind-boggling but frank.

Dayo actually dumped her in Africa without any form of notification. He left her heart broken.

'So sorry about that. So sorry. I did all I could but-'.

She holds her gaze for a moment, still wondering, mouth opened. Is she in a kind of perpetual dream or boundless imagination requiring instant liberation? *This can't be real. This cant be happening to me.* She loses control of her sentiments and waves of gloom, grief, treachery and despair sweep over her. Tears course down her cheeks.

'Oh my God. Labi, what happened? Didn't he inform you before he left?', Segun pretends not to know something. It's a promise he mustn't break, notwithstanding her turmoil. Only twelve days ago, he elucidated why he wouldn't find her till he left. He did all things imaginable, beseeched on her behalf, for consideration, but he already made up his mind. He asserted, in their closing dialogue, that he must quit hold of her and recompence her, in another way, after establishing himself in America. Quite unfortunate for the poor girl, he calculates, but he doesn't care about her. He worries much about his new life in a proposed marriage, and about Meghan and America. What should he do in a situation where his hands are tied? Now, his projection that she will come and fish for information, only from him, has materialized. In no circumstances should he disclose the truth.

'He didn't tell me anything. He didn't tell me it was time to leave. He supposed to, at least, see me before leaving. Oh-God, humans are so wicked. Why did Dayo treat me like this?', she weeps on. At the same time her cries magnetizes Soronje from the kitchen, Segun rises to console her.

'What is going on? Sister Labi, why are you crying?' she stays within spitting distance, suitable enough to mind her business. Wiping her hands with a napkin, her face falls in compassion, her fully grown pregnancy thrusting against a springy dress. Despite her wordiness, she is a respecter of ground rules: earth-shattering rules in her life. She will rather shut her mouth and protect her affair than become an object too. Extreme talk is now a constraint to avert unseasonable termination of her stay. She must watch her step; else she will be stepped upon. Segun turns and gives her a warning signal with only his eyes and she understands. She prepares her mind for only one evocative statement to make and disappear into her room.

'Sorry- sister Labi. Sorry'. She walks away slowly, now making her way to the kitchen, to eavesdrop on their conversation. He doesn't care wherever she goes, so long she's out of sight. She must learn not to pry in people's affair or let him be. He looks over his shoulder to observe her presence then continues to comfort her.

'Labi- You don't have to cry. The lord is with you, the lord is your strength. God will replace him with the best of men. The one that will be yours forever. God will bring him. Don't cry', he pulls her closer, leans her head on his shoulder. She cries on. His prayers are like a destructive disease in her ears. No more prayers or there will be more disaster. *What do you mean replace? What about Dayo? Has he ended our relationship? Oh God, how will I survive without him? Why?*

Soronje pulls a long breath, having gathered the heart of the matter. It's incredible he departed after taking full advantage of her. Is it by luck she got Segun? Will he still throw her away like an orange peel after sucking the juice? She drops the frying pan in her hand and rests on a cabinet. Her hesitant mind set in. *Is it by chance I got impregnated by this fool? What if he does the same thing to me? It will be worse if he deserts me with a baby. What will be my gain? They are birds of a feather, that's why they are friends for a long- long time. I will never let this happen to me. Ever!* She slams the pan against the wall, Segun looks in her direction. Again, she creeps into the room.

At the same time, she begins to strategize on making him stay forever. She won't let that happen to her, not with a baby. Moving on with another man's baby is even tougher, she agrees, deep in thought. Angered, she ruminates on his claim to produce a child before marrying her: an antiquated condition she came to terms with to win his heart. She breaks into a laughter of retribution, pauses and shakes her head in sheer pity. *Is it fair to do all that for nothing?* Now she understands why he still will not tie the knot with her after all is said and done. They probably had an agreement to always use and dump their lovers. Come what may, she is ready for him.

'Labi, believe me, he can't forget you. He is coming back for you. I believe. He loves you', he wipes her tears with his napkin. 'And trust me-', he adds. 'I won't stop talking to him until he comes for you'.

Labi sniffs, cries and turns to ask him an astounding question. 'Do you have his number abroad? I have to talk to him.'

'What?', confusion clouds his face. Is that a proof that he is forgiven? Why is she demanding for his number, despite her misery? With that, he believes that she will never give up on him, no matter the distance.

'Yes- he must have called you- his friend- after he got there. Please, I beg you in God's name, to give me his number', she pleads amidst sobs.

'His number?', he quickly plans a response. Soronje gives a grimace of irritation. She thought it out well, they are birds of a feather. She overheard them chatting in their living room just yesterday. Why can't he give the number now? *Segun is a traitor!* She wraps her arms above her belly, leans on the cabinet to hear his response, head tilted slightly to one side.

He rises to his feet, paces around the room, deliberating over her request. He won't betray him or give the game away by providing his number. Rather, he will choose to call on her behalf and still plead with him. He sneaks a look at her, frowns at her steadfastness. If he says it is over, it is certainly over. *Why will she force herself upon him especially now that he is far away? And when he has married another woman. Besides, he is not the only man in the world. This girl is crazy. Very crazy. And I won't let her ruin my relationship with my friend.* What about Meghan? Any upsetting call from a distressed ex may ruin his papers abroad or trigger his deportation. He still needs her to become a resident in the U.S, so he should be careful at this time. In the light of his consideration, he turns her down.

'Labi, I don't have his number', he says finally, striding back to her. Soronje wraps her hands behind her head, shocked at his response. She is beginning to know how much her darling can beat about the bush to save his hardhearted friend. *What a shame!*

'He called only once and- that was six days ago with his neighbor's number. He said he doesn't have a phone yet. And you know it's wrong to call his neighbor. He is a white', he clarifies, smiling. He sits down, relaxes his back on the sofa next to her, his fingers tapping, acceding a guilt complex. At the same time, he commends his heroic friend for making it, against all odds. Now, the sky is the limit. He admits that in less than no time, Labi will forget about him and move on too.

'Labi, forget about him. Tell me about your school project. Wow! You will soon become a graduate and get a good job- ride a nice car and-' he tries to divert her attention from him, make her see the brighter side of her future. Soronje sizes up the air. *Are you kidding me?*

When she begins to talk about her school programme, towards her final year, she slows down the tears. Her eyes are reddish and swollen, nose congested. She sniffs from time to time, in the middle of her conversation.

'Listen to me. You have a brighter future ahead of you. Don't kill yourself for a man. I am now talking to you as my sister. If a woman kills herself for a man, thousands of men will spit on her grave. A broken pre-marital affair is better than a broken marriage. An eye that will last long with you will not discharge at its earlier stage. Labi, think about it. You are educated, bold, strong and beautiful. You have it all. Be free, forget about him', he looks straight in her eyes. Her gaze lowers in shame and desolation. What else would she say to him? Thanks? She pulls a long sigh, rubs her face with the back of her hands and prepares to leave.

'Brother Segun, I have to go now. I really appreciate your support. Thank you so much', she rises from her seat, the fluff in the sofa rising along, breaking free from her deep pressure. It puffs an air of relief watching her go. She looks around for Soronje who deceitfully absorbs in nonexistent chores in her kitchen. She feels sorry for her, wanted to be a shoulder to cry on but her restraint keeps her away. In spite of this, she knows she will still assist her one day.

'Won't you at least, eat something before you leave? My wife is preparing breakfast. Let's all dine together', he smiles, peering straight in the kitchen. He sees Soronje's hand next to the refrigerator.

This nosy woman will never change. Take a look at her, carrying her busy body around. He who falls in a pit teaches others a lesson. We shall see how your life turns out in this affair if you don't modify your ways. I will just run and leave you with your problems. If Labi is dumped, who are you?

'I will keep in touch. Thank you so much', Labi opens their entrance door. A ray of sunlight hits her face, a chill still around the air. She freezes, wraps her arms around herself. With that, she compares two sensations of life: hot or cold. As weather changes, so situations vary. Things will never remain the same. We must always prepare for changes in life.

'I will get his real number and text it to you', Segun remains at his door. He has just a pair of shorts on, can't step outside. He wraps up their conversation very quick then closes his door slowly, rather less spirited than when he just set his eyes on her.

Its irrefutable that she senses a new life around her. Dayo is gone, she is by herself. As Segun said, life goes on. With her existence, she stands the chance of stepping up higher in life. She learnt her lessons bitterly, will use it to strengthen her weakness. If she dies, her hope ends with her, her dreams unaccomplished. She will survive, move on.

Right away, she begins to plan an engrossing project: a long-term task requiring her attention and barring her mind from a fugitive lover. Life goes on. She won't give up on herself or her life for a man that cares nothing about her. She's worth more than that.

9

L ABI CURLS UP WITH her pillow, tosses around in an antique bed, of a low-cost hostel, in the suburban area. For six hours now, she has been in the same position, moping on her earth-shattering experience, her presumptive moves over her head. He broke her heart; she feels a thousand grave digger delving deep in her soul. She wants to give up on life- for life itself occurs lifeless, so vacuous without a thing that raises her spirits. Insofar as she tries to blank it out and draw a new beginning, she fails. She is deteriorating in all ways; she knows, she is upside down viewing her subsistence thousands of miles away. What happens to those pledges and drives? Did they also vanish with him, all lost at once? She quivers, makes an effort to forget but feels cumbersome, his perfidy so enormous, too indelible in her thought.

Her bed suddenly turns a cohort, her pillow the comforter, scarcely departing her arms. Now, she likes it dark, every illumination rebuilds memories of a lost equitable hope. Not too much of talking around her or she is driven over the edge. It's simply tough to say that, seeing Dayo ends the state of affairs.

She feels a sharp pain around her abdominal region and

grimaces. Her hurting stomach growls out of displeasure, bereft of food, starved of all its accustomed care inside-out. Her mind takes charge of everything: her entire wellbeing. If its frail, she's fruitless. She rolls over her stomach, burrows deeper in the bed, and cultivates more fervor for undeserving devastation.

Her relationship with friends and families has also changed. She scarcely relates with course mates in school, doesn't want time with her mum and siblings. Unlike before, she appears dull and passive and plumps either for solitude or vagueness. But for the superfluous yowling that visits without warning, seclusion and soliloquy seem more effective than socializing. She wants to be by herself-to properly create a mental image of her beloved- to see him even though he is not there physically.

Tolu, her roommate, understands her predicament. She battles with forced fellow feeling- and hardly sleeps at night- or rests in the daytime. Labi cries almost all the time, repeating only two words: *why me, why me, why me?* This is sickening. She wishes she had another place to go. Sometimes, empathy subdues her intents, and she joins in with her hourly sobs; at another time, she turns irritable. Even though she can't sincerely tell if Dayo will return to her or not, her unconquerable assertions will. She has to say or do something to sustain her, save her from self-destructive conceptions or going down the tubes. Only two days ago, she took it upon herself to find him. Who knows if he's around and hiding from her? On arrival, a young auto mechanic turned up. He didn't have the faintest idea who she inquired about. He has long disappeared without notice. So sad for poor Labi, too bad for her. As far as she is concerned, Dayo is undisturbed about her bestie, doesn't have any care in the world.

Five minutes after, a harsher pain stings. She rolls over the edge of her bed, clutching a spot, drumming continuously to alleviate the pain. Her eyes fall on a meal Tolu prepared earlier that morning, disinterestedly. Who knows? Miracle may push it down her throat, into her belly. As she advances upon it, she gets sidetracked by a voice from within, got reminded of her beloved in a new home-around a new life. She withdraws instantly, falls back in her bed with all secreted emptiness, her hands around her head. She begins to cry again.

'Hey babe, you are hurting yourself badly. This is not good for you. Do you wish to die? This is too much. You are so crazy. Very crazy', Tolu barges in on her. She attended the morning lecture alone: three tests written, projects submitted, assignments graded but nothing draws her attention to her studies at the moment. Like a joke, her scores declined to 2point, dropped to 1.5 the previous week. She fears she would have to re- take that academic year albeit she resigned herself to failure. The last result shows lots of 20s and 30s, unlike her regular 80s and 90s. She feels she now revels in abysmal catastrophe. It is difficult; however, she is willing to get her into shape.

'Omolabi! Did you check your appearance in the mirror today? You are so ugly now. Too ugly and unsightly for a friend. You are embarrassing yourself. Who cares about this your useless love? You missed another test today, five tests- to be precise! You keep failing every time and if you're not careful- I mean, if you don't stop acting this way, I will bring your mum into this. You are affecting my life with your mood. I can't enjoy my final year in this school, why? I need to know why?'. She walks across her legs and proceeds into the room. She screws up her face, then closes her eyes to her irritation. That's what she intends to do-avoid her all the time and yield a positive result. When she's absolutely ignored, she will be tired. What does she know about love? Has she ever been loved before?

She pictures herself living a loveless life as her helpful friend, Tolulope. She thinks she is luckier. She is not the one suffering the pain right now. Her life feels better, she is focused on her studies- no misfortune allowed in her life. Since she is quiet and engrossed with her computer right now, she decides to mind her step. She wanted to deal with it till the time she finds another place to go but cannot hold on for long. Sobs emerge in stages, coughs, pause and raucous.

Tolu sighs, drops her computer with full-fledged infuriation. Tired and short of words, she crosses her legs and watches her for a moment. Her head declines in pity then rises for another moment of bitter truth. 'You know what Labi? You are going to waste yourself away for nothing. The earlier you admit now that life continues, the better for you. Believe me, he's going to marry someone in America- and look at you here!', she waves her hand from her ruffled hair down her body, contemptibly, her lips curling in disdain.

'If you don't look good for better men to see you, everyone- everybody will think you are suffering from mental illness. You don't look right. I mean, who will stay with a depressed woman?! He has left you already. Stop disturbing me. You will not make me cry for you tonight. Never again!'.

'He can't leave me. He will return. He will', she flounders in self-assurance still weeping. Tolu draws a breath too long for her wellbeing, weighs up a better option before she loses her mind too. She has home works to do- discourse analysis takes two hours while literary appreciation takes approximately four hours. At 7pm, she needs to visit a neighboring grocery store, then find time to call her family to request for her monthly support. And the cries that visit her ears like flies to a wound. There is hardly any more time to waste around infected snuffles. Speedier than a lightning flash, her bag dismounts a wooden rack above her bed. She fills it up in burst of anger, slams her backpack in readiness to leave, then pauses to find her shoes and wallet. All set, she bags her computer and leaves the room, slamming the door behind her.

She smells an air of happiness outdoors. Labi drains her with her pointless nightmare. *Dayo this, Dayo that. What the hell?!* Now twenty-nine, she doesn't believe in true love after she grew up in a broken home. She is raised to believe in herself and depend largely on love from within. Outward love is futile, misleading. After the trauma she suffered in her childhood, she is determined never to love or possibly stay unmarried forever. On top of that, she witnesses her friend's disconsolate life in her youthfulness. She is under the illusion that love doesn't exist, nevertheless super people make it work.

10

SORONJE SINGS OVER A piercing scream from her infant. At four months, Bolanle looks robust, so full of life, her frequently adorned head a mass of black curly hair, brushed backwards in style. She bears a resemblance to her father with her small mouth and round nose, Soronje thinks she has her skin color. There is warmth, stillness and a leisurely examination of her new habitat, in a snug shawl, neck and face peeping, eyes tightened. A moment comes when she's propelled to request for one thing and another bawling. In slow progression, she kicks off with a jumpy cough that evolves into the shrillest cry that moves a mountain. She kicks out at her tidy wrap and throws her limbs in the air for urgent care. It's a new life her parents are accustomed to except for her night-time ruckus that seems never to end. At thirty-one, Segun lives with his first baby: a privilege brought about by a sudden turn of events, except for all the troubles on the horizon. To the best of his belief, Bola is not just a baby but a replication of who he can single out in the dark. She is genetically inflexible and noisy like her mother. All the same, Soronje accepts the animosity caused by her newborn even though it's always written on his face.

Most time, Segun is spotted sneaking a look at the

infant rather than helping to lull her. He gives excuses when they take turn to drive her to sleep, goes berserk for overmuch noises. Its either he is tired, or he needs some rest before dawn. From every indication, he detests the coming of his child. He has a mirror that reflects his true image to him every day, and it never occurred to him that there is a slim likeness between him and Bola. He has never thought, and he won't think for once, that they look alike-in anyway.

'Can this baby be quiet for once? I didn't get enough sleep last night, ah', he darts off the sofa in the sitting room. Soronje ignores him. At the same moment, he starts bemoaning admitting her in his life. Through her, another trouble has emerged undeniably. He doesn't like both mother and child. Before she was born, he presumed a love child, probably around to restore his lost hope. But she came with another stumbling block. He thinks she's as uninviting as her mum- she appears too old for her age and too dark for him. *Do I hate babies? No, its different with all the babies I've seen in my life.* And why does he despise her that much? He questions his willful abhorrence more often than not. All babies he has seen came with a sham fair color that fades away afterwards but Bola came black-too dark for what he envisioned before she was delivered. He dreamt of a smooth baby with a nice smile, not what he sees now daily. With her bad nutrition, she altered his dream, maybe. Her whole face is masked off from admiration with immedicable rashes that emerges at first sight. Seeing her, he presumes a waste of resources as his money succumbs to some provocative powder and badly bottled food.

When Soronje set her on the same sofa he vacates, he gets wrathful. He peeks through the door and sees the baby's face. She feels more confident in herself, relaxes and delights in his departure. As long as he is gone, they are both happy. Now feeling extremely displeased, his unsettled mind leads him back to the living room. She still ignores him. She carries her baby and continues singing, watching her suckle from her anxiously. Segun paces around, unhappy they occupy his position in the room, against his wish. He thinks of a way to get even with them then says, ' why do you sing that song to the baby? Why? It doesn't sound good at all. Why that song?' he takes the position adjacent her, nursing his goatee. She shot him an angry stare then looks down at her busy baby. She knows he doesn't like them both, has always shown the feelings to them. The genuine truth is that he wants to kick off an argument at a wrong time with her. *What more should I worry about?* Recently, her business isn't flourishing like before. Since Bola was born, there isn't enough supervision and monetary support she requires, hence her resources cripple all along- time after time. This saddens her, especially when she's unaided.

'Segun, I sing to silent the child. Can you please spare us today? I have too much on my mind'. She hisses, continues humming.

'Even when she smiles, do you still need to sing?'

'What exactly do you want? What are you talking about?', she yells, and he won't stop. He is prepared to frustrate her out of his home. He recently found a new love like his friend, can't wait to kick her out with her baby. And they both disgust him

'Listen- mum', he sneers, then continues, ' we both

want her to speak the Queen's English, so why sing to her in your language?'

'What do you mean?', she looks dumbfounded, searches her mind for the basis of his argument. *Is he okay?* 'I can sing to her in any language I know. She's my child and I want her to speak my language. I am proud of my language', she cuts in abruptly, rises with the baby still suckling.

'Impolite- barbaric and inexcusably disrespectful. The baby will soon grow up to talk like you. Soonest there will be two parrots in this house'. He rises along with them. Soronje gets more exasperated being ill-treated with an infant. There is always a way out of his abuse but for the guiltless one and her patriarchal needs, she put the heat under control.

She cuddles her sleeping baby and closes her door gently. Segun follows them. He won't give up till they grab their stuff and leave him alone. Only a tone from his phone deters him from progressing. His face cracks into a startling smile, seeing the call. He relaxes in the sofa, chats exhaustively with Dayo. Soronje pays close attention to him.

'Congratulations on your wedding ceremony. I wish you a happy married life. At last- you live in the US, thank God', he sits down. Soronje walks past him to check the door. Without a nodding acquaintance with the visitor, she throws the entrance open like a bull at a gate. He gets scared, prepares for resistance. He rises, fixes his eyes on the door. Recently his neighbor suffered an armed robbery attack and he's robbed of all his belongings. He was left black and blue when he bristled at the onslaught. Now in the hospital, he lies dead to the world receiving medication.

Eniola. F. Fagbemi

Labi walks into the room smiling. Segun ends the call instantly. He made a vow he mustn't break, come what may. He stands at the center of the living room unleashing a welcoming smirk, the other side of him questioning her steadfastness and Soronje's absurdities. His phone begins to ring again, he ignores it. By no stretch of the imagination could anyone say she hasn't accepted her fate. She appears as pleased as punch, more confident in herself than the last time she came looking dejected. He calculates her mission in their home again. For sure, he knows she isn't there for Soronje, him or their newborn. She has returned to fix her broken heart again, probably try her luck once more. She will not give up until she gathers her heart together, considering how much she loves him. His love dwells in her heart, rules her head, dominates her mind and affects her soul. It's all over her- she still loves him now and forever. He wishes he had that, from a woman he loves equally- a woman that has it all: bold, beautiful and intelligent. Not the like of Soronje. He turns toward her and sizes her up. At that hour of the day, she is bedraggled, hasn't taken a shower, to at least clean the spot the baby suckles from.

'You look so radiant. I love your outfit and your make up', Soronje breaks in his thought, Labi flashes a radiant smile. He smirks absent-mindedly. Sooner, his phone begins to ring. It is Dayo. He ended the call in the middle of an important discussion. *I must explain the reason for my sudden disconnection, else...he needs to know that she's back.* He lowers his gaze on the phone to send an explanatory message. Soronje, in turn, sizes him up. For the past three months, before she delivered their child, he has been receiving a hole in the corner calls, locking himself up and texting messages for a period too inconvenient in a bathroom. At another time, he would ignore her, stick to social media and chat for hours. When he sees her coming, he flips his phone over. She can't touch his devices; he locks them with strange dot lines and passwords. She knows it, without being told, that her husband flirts, keeps secret affairs. His side chic is calling, maybe. Her mood changes instantly. She welcomes Labi once more and leaves them alone in the living room.

'Please, have a seat', he ushers her to a comforting spot on their sofa.

'Thank you so much', she smiles from ear to ear, removing her floral embroidery mini crossbody bag, and sitting elegantly. Yes, the sad times are over. She brushed up and started over again. Segun takes another look at her. Her enormous beauty glows-it takes his breath away, sweeps him off his feet. Of all the six ladies he just met, no one looks that stunning. There is something unique about her look: her facial attraction and physique, perhaps. The earlier her old feelings tail off the better for her resplendent appearance.

'I see- you have forgotten about my friend. You have somebody now, maybe', he teases her, looking down and texting with his phone. He should be informed about what he just saw, after all, they talk about her all the time.

'That's not true. I'm trying, I'm really trying but I can't just forget about him- like that. I have a friend that's helping me get over the trauma and'.

'She's doing a great job, he cuts in abruptly, looks up at her then continues texting. 'She has brought you back to life and I'm happy for you', he sends the message and looks up at her.

A smirk is transfixed on her face. She looks around for a while then asks, 'how is your baby?' It was the first thing she cared to ask Soronje about, but she seemed perturbed by something, judging from the times she caught them both sharing hostile glances.

'Yes, I sent out a message to inform all my friends on Facebook when she was delivered, and I decided to give you some time. I didn't know if you were angry with me too or- you were still broken then', he chooses his words wisely, carefully.

'It's alright, can I see her now?' she prepares to carry her, drops her crossed legs. She has to conceal her pursuit with something different. It's a secret that she's there for her estranged lover. Segun shot an unrestrained angry stare at the baby's room. *Why can't she just mind the reason she is here? Why is she bringing double trouble around here? If her life matter doesn't count to her, I will be glad to leave them alone.* While he ponders on calling her right away, she asks him surprisingly, 'are you hearing from your friend?' her smile vanishes.

'Who? Dayo? Yes- he called me a week ago and -Soronje! Soronje!!', he interrupts thinking of what to say. Now, he chooses Soronje over her impending question. It's always overwhelming. He rises from the seat.

'And what?', she questions earnestly, her worried eyes on him.

'This woman heard me calling, didn't she?', he re-joins rather, deflecting from a direct response to her question. A cooked-up lie crosses his mind. He will neither betray his friend nor tell her about his success story.

'Sister! Sister!!', she helps him call her fondly and she

responds. She pauses for a moment then asks him the same question, 'What did he tell you about me?'

Oh my God. Why are ladies too docile in a wasted relationship? Can't she forget about him? For God's sake, he abandoned you in Africa for a new life, don't you understand? What does she expect me to say? That he divorced his wife to take you overseas? Oh, spare me!

He finally makes up his mind to counsel her, not as a friend but a sister. *Truth is acidic but must be communicated.*

'Labi- my darling sister- you already moved on. Please, keep moving on. Keep moving on. Try to forget about him. Consider your life, consider your future. If he doesn't care, then why should you? Love is fifty-fifty, not one-sided. To be sincere, he is married to another woman in America', he lets the cat out of the bag, unknowingly. He senses an unchallenged air of betrayal and defeat but didn't mind. She needs to give up on him. It is over between them. Her mood changes- all energy and luster calling in a moment earlier desert her face without a second thought. She bites her lips and wears a woe- be -gone look. And he proffers a presumed ultimate healing.

'Okay-alright. That's fine, I have moved on too-long ago', she snaps her fingers, swallows the clog in her throat to control her emotion and perfect her lies. She suppresses a whimper that proves her wrong. If truly she moves on, she needs to gather herself together. She breaks into a quizzical smile, manages her true feelings.

When he proceeds with his advice, Soronje enters the room. She turns a blind eye to her hubby's deceits. With her extravagant smiles and interest, she disregards his disheartening attitudes, directs her attention to their visitor and then modifies her wrongs before him. He doesn't care anyways. He keeps a weather eye open for her usual monstrosities, watching out for more flaws to display. Nothing about her interests him.

'How are you- sister? I am happy for you. You are smiling today. Let me get the baby. You will smile more. She is incredibly beautiful like you'. Soronje hurries back inside, wriggling her waist. Segun casts his gaze on the ceiling consistently. His mind has wandered off towards his busy day- a frantically scheduled day. In the next two hours, he resumes work for an eight-hour evening shift. When he closes, he visits a neighboring automated teller machine to withdraw for payment of his bills and deliver a weekly monetary support to his aged parents. At night, he wants to visit his girlfriend and spend some time with her. As her image reflects in his mind, he rises from his seat.

'Labi, I'll be right back. Give me just a few minutes, I'll be back to talk to you', he examines her sullen mood still. She nods and forces a smile. He comes across Soronje and the baby on the way. Now, she covers her whole face and neck with a methylated powder, her reddish eyeballs standing out like an abrasion on a black knee. She has an unsmiling face as usual and the smell of a strange cognac fills the air. He bends and twist to make way. *The sooner you guys are gone, the better for me.*

Soronje smiles into the living room, happy that he has given a chance to talk. As much as she wished to gossip with her the last time, she had no slightest chance to pour out her burning clues. Now, the opportunity finally emerges, in absence of a hateful hubby.

'Here, this is my baby. Isn't she as pretty as you are?',

she pushes Bola in her hands. She casts a suspicious look at Labi's face, winces and makes to follow her mother. She grabs her blouse, struggles to hold on.

'She is pretty. She is indeed a beauty. Look at her hair, so full', Labi rubs her hair to the back, the only thing she finds attractive. She nurses a different thought in her mind. *Is this the way I look? Never, she doesn't look anything akin to beauty. What an ugly baby!*

When she begins to cry, she looks very unsightly and she hands her to her mother.

'Keep quiet! What is wrong with you? You reject everybody- every time. Am I the only one in the world?', she hisses.

'It's okay, she is just a child. She loves her mum, and she knows you the most. Babies feel unsafe with strangers', she corrects her wrong notion but not absolutely.

'Including her father?'

'It's okay', Labi pauses, swallows hard, drawing a point from her argument. Are people avoiding her or she is avoiding people? She isn't there for either of them or a discourse concerning that, however she has to fake it. She stretches her hands to carry her again and she refuses, this time clutching firmer to her mother.

'She will be fine. She will get over this when she is like six months old. My niece was like that till she turned eight months', she lies to hearten her.

Soronje looks from angle to angle and leans over to whisper her mission to her.

'When are you less busy? I need to see you and tell you what you need to know about your boyfriend in America'.

'I can give you a call', she sits up with much more interest than she envisioned.

'Take my number', she watches her take her number quickly and saves it on her phone. When their tete a tete is complete, she raises her voice to wind up her visit.

'it's a pleasure having you around'. She winks at her, Labi plays along.

'I must take my leave now. I have an appointment at 4pm. I need to prepare before the class', she rises, crosses her bag around her body. Soronje walks inside to inform her husband but he is already in the shower. Labi sneaks a look at her, catches her eavesdropping on him. She shakes her head pitifully then proceeds towards the door.

For a reason, God has brought them together, but she doesn't sense love in the environment. In her short period of stay, she senses betrayal, deception, cheating, cynicism and hatred. It won't last long- not an inch close to what he had with Dayo. *Their relationship will hit a rock and Bola will suffer it all. She will be raised with no paternal love.*

'Never mind if he's busy. I have to go now. I will call him later', she opens the door, the sunbeam hits her face. Soronje hurries after her. She will be a good sister; something keeps reminding her of how compassionate she will be to her. She must help revitalize a lost faith in an unfeeling man. To her, all men are the same. Segun ill-treats her just like Dayo did to Labi. They can be helpful to themselves if she confides in her. She will tell her all she needs to know about him in America, and the future of their relationship.

'I will call you'

'Please do. I have a lot to tell you', she whispers smiling. She turns back in the room and closes the door. Labi begins her journey back home leisurely, her mind occupied with the thought of Segun's unequivocal declaration. Now, she knows why he left without a hint- he abandoned her to get married to the same woman he read about on his phone. She bit her lips, regretting not taking a quick action before he vanished. She had the prospect at her fingertip when he was much around, but she misused it. She breaks into a dull smile.

She walked past a glass door of a store and sees her unanticipated transformation. Within the short period she was there, her face dropped, the spirited drive she took in the apartment slackens and she looks so morose. What's going on with her again? Is she back to being gloomy or raking over the ashes after all Tolu did to bring her back to life? Unbelievable. She decides not to go straight to her apartment.

She must cool off her smarting emotion somewhere before heading home, else Tolu will call her mother again. That will be pepper upon injury, hearing the tale of how her father abandoned her years back. She sighs and headed towards an eatery. There, she plans to get a bottle of soda and wile away the time, probably on a call to a friend. Life is worth living well, existence is futile in a loveless atmosphere. A bargained love is worth the price of acceptance and endurance. A deceptive love, it's counterpart, appears like a thief in the night, rips the heart apart and vanishes with hope and expectation. The road to retrieval is rocky, hard and rough and full of distrust. And a lingering heart builds the path to failure and abhorrence. It's what she suffers now. She won't let go, or let in. Though ended, her faith remains that what has gone can still return- to stay and never elope again. *He is fiercely mine forever, I strongly believe.*

A GE IS A COMPELLING reality, a fundamental tool
domineering man's mind and actions. There is an
occasion for every pace it takes - a phase to crawl, toddle
and march to excel: beginning from birth and the last of
breath. A skin is savored to favor the time, the heart thuds
against our odds. The end of a year perplexes the mind,
reminds of yet another day away. A countdown lingers till
end of time. It rouses with the day and banquets with the
night-each day counts for living memories. It's made for
deification, evolution and love. To love to hate and hate to
love. The longer it lasts, the more chances of subsistence,
to unveil and prevail, blemish the unblemished and amend
the fragmented: conjoining the future with the present to
wipe off the past.

Labi struggles with the effect of age on her inner mind.
There is time for all things in life, especially in the African
society. The time arrived to make a choice, make hay while
the sun shines, yet no choice. It is now two years since
Dayo left her, still no replacement. She is afraid to move on,
thinking through the aftermath of her decision. She comes
to an assumption that if nothing happened to him when
he abandoned her and moved on, then she is free as well.

As a graduate, her mother expects her to, at least, introduce a suitor. Days roll by and neither a boyfriend nor a husband surfaces. Every time she tells the same old story of a man she expects to return from overseas. Irrevocably, she made up her mind to take a daring step and defeat the fear she harbored in her heart in the past years. It is now time to take the bull by the horn.

Since the last time she left Segun's apartment and spoke to Soronje, she chose never to return there again. Only there is where she harvests her misery and falls back where she slides. If she wants to move on, she really has to move on, regardless of all the distractions around her. Really, she understands she needs a new relationship to forget him absolutely, but she isn't one of those that give in to failure easily. Now two years after her futile effort, she brushes herself up and tries again.

For the third time, the soothsayer looks up at Labi from the scattered seeds on his mat then back to the seeds with sinking feeling. Once more, he collects the seeds from his oracle mat, joggles them in his fists and tosses them on the mat, uttering incantations, invoking the spirit of wisdom. He slows down, examining a disclosure with bird's eye view.

Labi feels her heart trembling, looking around the setting. She sees everything traditional around her, things she hasn't seen in her entire life. Seeing is believing- she only saw these in tv dramas and now she sits face to face with a herbalist, supported by Soronje. She sits next to her, a heartening smile registered on her face. She has known him for a long time, has been there a couple of times to twist the eyes of fate and fulfill the unfulfilled. To her, life is worth fighting and living for.

'Ehm-uhn', the small man in his mid-seventies clears his throat for a flawless delivery. It is time to relate his messages from the oracle, as he has puzzled out for the past sixty years of his lifetime. He knows the *orisha*, their favorite names and placation. These are the deities he venerates with great conciliation to attain a goal - then gives his glorification in return. It is his tradition, cultural curative and a dig into the future- an unbending world of reality. Labi, still does not believe in him, despite the little magic he saw in the communal transportation. To her, miracle doesn't exist except a make-believe return of a lost heart.

'Are you the one involved?', he points his spiritual horn at Labi.

'Yes, wise one, I am-', she kneels before him nervously. She has no idea what he is capable of but has gathered lots of stories about their spiritual potentialities. If they can make things work enigmatically, then they deserve that much admiration.

Soronje is astounded- she watches and breaks into a sardonic smile. Baba is her very close friend. With him, she triumphed in many dangerous undertakings and will forever be indebted to him. His place is distinct from her ardent position in her church. There is nothing she will do without him.

'Sit down, don't be afraid. I take care of your sister, I'll take care of you too', he points at the edge of a tatty mat she occupied earlier. He follows all her disconcerted moves till she is finally seated, legs outstretched, bag nuzzled up against her belly. A part of her condemns her presence in the scene, the other a nostalgia for her choices. Once more, he clears his throat then begins to divulge what he saw. He widens his eyes unequivocally, mutters some impenetrable words and looks up at her.

'That man you want to marry is in trouble. He is in soup'.

'Soup? Can you please explain that?', Soronje speculates.

'Yes, because he is enchanted and tied down with a padlock. You can wait and expect him for hundred years, he will never return to you. Someone has won him over', he stares at Labi raptly. He confuses her, and she nurses mixed feelings: a sense of dispossession and despondency. As levelheaded as she presumed to be, she feels luckless and neglectful allowing someone to take what is rightly hers, even though she tried her best. And she is dogged to fight for it now.

'He will never return by himself except you do something', he echoes, looking from Soronje to Labi, his eyes on her bare shoulders. She adjusts her off-the-shoulder top awkwardly and bites her finger in remorse. Had she known it was the circumstance, she would have tussled with her rival. For a reason, her mind wanders on his last statement. If earnestly something can be done to fix her worries, then there is a way out. Suddenly, she frets more about the upshots than the problem itself. The harm is done already but there is a sure way out.

'If I can fiercely make him mine forever, then what is the way out?', she says apologetically, to Soronje's surprise, almost falling on her knees again. The old man looks at her with much pity. In her eyes, he sees genuine and perpetual love. She will love him till the end, notwithstanding the situation. True love lives in her heart. But danger still prowls behind them. He isn't done yet. He prepares himself to disclose the risks awaiting him for breaking a vow.

'There was a covenant between you and this man-and that's the reason you don't want to leave him', he gestures with his horn.

Soronje shot her a remarkable stare. For a moment, she stops trusting her and keeps her ears opened for more startling awes of love. Little wonders she becomes so agitated about the details she gathered from her. Why did she lift the part of their covenant? She holds her gaze until she begins to confess to the wise one.

'Is it still effective and persuasive? We did that a long time ago', she utters with regret. What becomes of her destiny if he fails to return? Her stare drops on the oracle mat; she shakes her legs in anguish. She admits she treacherously allowed her heart to rule her head.

Baba burst out laughing, a displaced front tooth unravels. It isn't long when it shut itself off their infiltrating eyes for usual seclusion. However, it isn't as relevant as the heart of the matter. He shakes his head constantly then looks at her in all honesty. *Do people in the computer age still do that? Quite surprising!*

'You children of nowadays know nothing. You take everything you see for granted. When you see someone do something, you also do it. That is why this life is turning upside down. That thing you did is still in effect'.

Labi looks flushed. She thought it lost its potency when he left, she is surprised it's still in effect.

'What do I do wise one? Help me', she falls on her knees yet again.

'Sit down. Are you begging to help yourself or the man?'

'Both of us- both of us', she looks confused, looks at Soronje's face. She portrays the same gesture of pity as the old one then turns away from her. From then, she sees her differently. She appears to her as a love fanatic - she can crucify herself to win a heart.

'That's dangerous. Whoever breaks the vow will go blind and-', he surveys the outcome, dispersing the seeds. 'You did not break the vow, but he did'. He concludes. Both of them understood what it meant. They fixed their gazes on the tool disclosing their secrecies: the third eye only the old one can use. Labi is wordless, Soronje falls in deep thought. *Hmmn! Wonders shall never cease, even in this computer age.* Having said all he has seen, he wraps his bony legs together, anticipates their needs. Soronje sneaks a look at Labi from time to time. Now, her head is buried in her hand. She is at a loss what to do. When she said nothing in a couple of seconds, she tables her opinion.

'Baba- bring him back home. Her problem is resolved when he is here. Besides, there is nothing he wants from there he cannot get from here. America- America -America. I don't know why everybody wants to be there. Our country is good too. Bring him back to her', she says ignorantly, irritably. Labi doesn't welcome the idea with her whole heart. Cutting off the head is not a cure for headache, there is surely a different alternative. As she attempts to refute her harsh thought, an idea strikes her, and she pauses.

'Is that what you want?'

'Yes sir. If I leave him there, he will still not be mine. I want him to be fiercely mine forever', she exchanges glances with Soronje in accord to her proposition. Leaving him there subdues her entire hope and puts her in risk of losing her sight in the future. He must return to Africa. *Simple.* The two desperate ladies whisper to themselves, ear glued to mouth. Baba busies himself with enquiry on executing their wishes. Using his third eye, he unearthed three different ways to accomplish their plans and only one seems to ring true. The other two put him at more risk of being unhappy in life. In the middle of his exploration, he pulls a long breath. *Oh God, how can a young man be in this much trouble? Is it now a problem to have a great look and great stars? The gains of a man is the fruit of his labor but not everything that glitters is gold. That is his luck, anyways. I have to do my job.*

'Woman, if you choose this one, its good. He will return home in seven days.

'Seven days? That is too long. Can't it be tomorrow?', Soronje requests, Labi casts a surprising look at her. *Really? Tomorrow? That's too quick. Shush sis, let me talk!*

He looks from Soronje to Labi, and back to Soronje. His eyes finally rests on her, since she determines how to live her life. If her assumption works, then that's what he will do. For a moment, she is lost. Does she really want to return him home, away from his splendor and finally rejoins with him or leave him alone to continue facing the wrath of their mindless oath? In state of dilemma, she sighs. Returning him home to her fingertip will be the best bet, if she must make the rightest choice. Other choices are useless except this, even the dumbest will accept this. She weighs the options. The herbalist fixes her with the same hard long anxious stare till she nods saying, 'Seven days will be fine. Let him return home in seven days. That way, he has a chance to plan for his life'.

'Okay', he sets to work immediately. He begins his indecipherable incantations. At a point, he stops and asks for the needful.

'What is his name again and do you have his photo?'

'His name is Dayo and I have this picture with me', Labi gropes for his youth service picture in her bag. She carries it all the time and feels the surge for his love. She feels the same way before handing it over. God knows how much she missed him. If by his power, he returns to her, she will be the happiest lady living on planet earth.

'This is a fine man. A good-looking man', he smiles at the photo, admiring his look and luck to be wanted by numerous great, beautiful ladies, at the same time. He never had such an opportunity in life.

'Leave the rest of the work for me. Your charge is two thousand and I will do a good job'.

'Thank you, sir. I will give you the money right away', she opens her wallet to pay him without negotiating. Soronje is sickened. They both live in a society where everything is bargained. Why the smugness?

'I have to warn you', he raised his hands for attention. They both pause and listen to him, his ample grey brow angling.

'You must return here to inform me immediately he returns. Don't waste time because it is dangerous. There are certain rites I must carry out to cast away the spell that brings him home. If you don't do that, he will be mentally deranged forever', his eyes widen emphatically. Soronje exchanges glances with Labi. Labi is horror-stricken.

Madness? God forbid evil! Is it safe to proceed? Her interest and trust in the charm goes downhill. She almost gives up her hope but for Soronje's interruption.

'That is not a problem. We shall return to inform you as you say. We will do whatever you need us to do to assist you. He is my husband's best friend and there is no day they don't gossip about something. I will keep her informed about his return'. She checks her watch and prepares to take her leave. Bolanle has been in her mother's care for approximately five hours now. She rarely gives her much trouble except for the time she stays out for too long and cries almost all the time. For once, she conceded that Bola is a little trouble. She rises from the mat and Labi follows. Her beloveds is traded to a stranger: to spiritually sway his life. It is time to go. Did she feel any regret, shame or betrayal whatsoever? No, she is delighted except for the tinge of fear in her heart and apprehension of the unknown. Only the one with the heart of a lion ventures spiritual mission to twist the eyes of fate and make the impossible possible, question the verity of life and reality. There, she stands bridging the guild against her primitive religious teaching, defying every restraining sermon. For the first time in her life, she tries out a new faith she believes would happen like a flash and fulfil her destiny in the twinkle of an eye. In the beginning, they had an agreement they both must fulfil whether he likes it or not. She rows the boat to their unfinished deal to protect them from life uncertainties and sorrow. What will be must be, she is ready.

'Baba, we will call you immediately we see a difference-any change at all, we will give you a call. We have to leave now because of my daughter', she leads the way, Labi follows. From then on, she opts to follow her lead.

'Thank you so much sir. I will also call you. I will collect your number from her. Goodbye sir'.

'Alright. He has nowhere to go without you. He will return in just seven days and you will be together again. He is fiercely yours forever', he laughs mockingly. His quivering finger runs into a hole in the wall accidentally, he touches the head of a cockroach. He peeks in and it scurries into a secret crack. He ignores it. Carcasses of animals, feathers of sacrificed birds, littered blood, and usual sanctification of the terrestrial invoke the attendance of apparently spine-chilling insects. They lodge in his dwelling, squint at all evil and good accounts, listen to success stories and diverse state of affairs of life. Not forgetting to acknowledge divinity for generating them in their forms, they glory in creation, hole up from evil, plaguing to displace from grace to grass in the name of love.

It is 5pm. The new besties set out for different destinations. Soronje walks faster, considering her mother's journey back to her home in the outskirt of the city on the same day. Besides, the presence of Segun in the same house with her churns her belly. She still doesn't comprehend why they despise themselves after all is said and done. She will return for that on another day, perhaps.

'Thank you so much Soronje. You are the best. This man wants to suffer me for nothing. Tell me where he wants me to start from. Where? 'Labi hastens to keep up with her quick gait.

'They are birds of the same feather. Segun is like that too. But for the help of Baba that holds him down for me, he lies too much. He planned to leave me long ago, but I thought fiercely mine is better'.

'Exactly. That teaches them a lesson'.

'Of course, my sister. Nothing goes for nothing'.

Almost approaching a bus station where a mini bus sits and hopes for arrivals, Labi shields her face from a piercing sun. On the face of it, she hinged upon something to restore her lost hope, faster than she envisaged. It is a memorable day in her life- a day she ventured a formidable act to fight for her heart. She feels a respite, for what she genuinely loves, she can't ignore. Finally, she expects his arrival by mystical forces. He shall return to shield her face from the sun, rub her back when it burns and speak for her when she is voiceless: just like the old time when they began their love journey. *He must continue where he stopped.*

At a location, the sun slows down, in prospect of a cooling atmosphere. Soronje enters the bus first, followed closely by her. A cool breeze arrives, brushing their faces, wafting through and easing off a burning sensation. It is relieving. *Same relief I feel when the storm is over.*

12

SORONJE IS STAGGERED BY a remarkable appearance. She drops in on the door the fifth time then returns to the bosom of her room, looking edgy. She embraces self-reproach and treachery, pictures her image aiming a reproachful finger at her. She flops down in her bed, next to Bola's dress, her face cupped in fused hands. Nothing disquiets her like the plausible outcome of their transgression. They bit off more than they could chew, went too far. Forewarned is forearmed, as the coming of a fatal war doesn't get to a wise cripple. Whenever she endeavors to slip away, she is steered by a compulsion to concur and hold on for a moment. Her arms slide behind her- she saunters around in deep thought, face raised. *Where will I tell Segun I am going on a Sunday? Why did Labi turn off her phone. And- that Baba's network is unreachable. Is it seven days yet? Oh God!* She wraps her arms around her head disconsolately.

When she breezes back in the living room, she meets the two allies having a tete a tete dialogue. From the look on his face, it is easy to tell that Segun is still dumbfounded, seeing Dayo bright and early, sitting in his old sofa, in the city of Canol, west Africa. Incredible! A couple of times, his eyes have tripped from his face down his toes in the middle of their conversation. He has heard all his ill-starred stories guiding him back but hasn't precisely seen the basis of his arrival. He is perplexed. He just faced a serious, unforeseen trauma, he knows. But how will he, at least, stabilize his emotion at the moment? He doesn't look right-his troubled head in quivering hands, eyes dropped on the floor-he cries from within. Again, Segun moves closer to him and throws a big hand of friendship around his shoulder.

'It's okay brother. I feel worst- I feel unhappy that this happened to you. But- we just have to accept as it is right now and try hard to move on with our lives. It's okay- life continues'. He squeezes his arm.

Dayo heaves a long sigh, then looking straight in his eyes, he says, 'Segun, do you know what that means? A death sentence or life imprisonment. And how could I have allowed that to happen? Segun, what hope is here? Nothing, nothing. Oh men! Why?' he cries finally, his shoulders wobbling in depression. Segun draws closer in fellow feeling. This is difficult for him. Dayo looks at him absently. Is he back in Africa? He sighs, wraps his arms around his head miserably. He watches his backpack lying on the floor then flashes back at the panicky scenario. His sense of guilt sets in, there is a cause and effect. Once more, he sees his autistic client battling with his last breath before fleeing from his house in Martin Boulevard, New York city. Doubling his pace and increasing his speed twice over the limit, he arrived home amidst a call to his closest friend in New York. And with his support, he found himself at an international airport in Africa.

'Oh! Segun, I'm in deep shit. Oh god! Why? Why was

I stupid to...', he hisses, bursts in tears. Segun is so down in the dumps. He pauses for a while then asks again, in his curiosity, 'how could you make such a mistake? Was it the first time you were assigned to that duty? Something is strange about the incidence', Segun breaks in his deep memory, his arms between his laps. When he looks up at him, he continues crying.

'No tears man, you have to be strong. You didn't plan to kill someone', Segun squeezes his shoulder sympathetically. He cries on, convulses with tears. Was it all about the dead client he was assigned to or infringing the American law? Overall, he absconded the wrath of law but stands no chance of ever gaining entrance into America again. *Damn!* He rises to his feet fiercely, heads to the wall and lands it three excruciating blows. Segun rushes to his rescue.

'Dayo, stop! Don't hurt yourself, the harm is done already. Don't complicate your issue. Please, I beg of you. Let us thank God in every situation. What if you were caught and sent to jail? You know what I mean? I don't live there but I learnt it is a lawful country. They don't kid with crime. You know what I mean- ten years, twenty years or even forever. Please- my friend'. He watches him slide to the floor, hit his head on the wall, continuously. He pins him down.

'Guy- guy, don't hurt yourself. Don't. If I found myself in this situation, I would rather choose to be alive and free than to be locked up. It's not the end of the world. We are here for you. When there's life, there is a sure hope. You have more chances in life. Your wife is there, your kid is there. Half of your life is still there'.

'Segun-Segun. I can't believe what happened. I just got my green card. I-', he cries on.

'It's okay man, it's not the end of the world. God still exists for you. At the end of every tunnel, there is a light', his heart sinks spotting his puffy and reddish eyes beclouded with tears. He cries his eyes out. Segun gets infected by his tears and feels a film of tears in his eyes too. He blinks it off at once. It's not the way he chooses to help out; it's not his way.

From the kitchen, Soronje watches them discreetly. She feels nothing akin to guilt or sympathy for them. It is just the beginning. *That punishment serves you right. In your life, you won't be cruel to someone that sold her heart and even her life to you. Wicked man- wicked men. You- Segun, your fate will be worse than ever if you try to leave me. You are fiercely mine forever or terrible till eternity. Shameless men, America my foot!* She hurries back to the backdoor to look at a long, lonely road. Labi's phone is still turned off, so she has no way to reach her and update her on the feasibility of their charm. Delay is dangerous as forewarned. In every way possible, they must arrange to see the priest. She claps her hands over her head, stamps her feet on the floor miserably. Its good they both thrived to drive him home but precluding the devastating effects is needful right now. Labi has also tried. Throughout the last three days, she called almost every time and they spoke at length. *What happened to her phone?! Oh God, this is not happening at the right time. I wish I had a chance to go out now and solve another trouble coming in this man's life.* All the time he sits there, she wishes she had a chance to leave the apartment and solve the unforeseen trouble coming his way. *If only your stupid friend knows what is coming for you, he will let me go*. She darts a fiery look at the entrance and storms in to make a request.

'Brother Dayo, you are welcome back. I hope you got some stuff for my daughter', she pretends not to have heard their conversation or why he returned home. Segun is infuriated. He sized her up, then yelled with a voice loud enough to wake the dead.

'I told you countless times to steer clear and shut your gab whenever I'm with my friends. Soronje, what do you want from me?!'

'Segun, are you guys fighting? That is too violent, take it easy- man', Dayo forces a response to quiet his rising rage. He knows everything about their relationship, he tells him everything- home or abroad. None of Soronje's secret is hidden. He knows she forced him into the relationship. And from their last conversation, before his arrival, he recollects all the uncovered voodoo secrets and hidden spots in the apartment. But for his pastor's admonition, he would have challenged her out of the house.

'This lady disgusts me with her barbaric style of living. She is uncultured and nasty. In short, she is a baboon in the zoo. I can marry a baboon instead of her', he waves his hand from her head down to her toe in sheer contempt. After he successfully puts her in the shade, she looks from him to his friend stupefied, heaves a long sigh and shakes her head. She never saw that coming.

'Oh God, what the hell? Segun, watch it, that's your wife? Seriously? You are incredible'.

'She is just a distraction. If she is pained, she can go in there and get her dirty stuff out of my apartment. She is not my wife, I didn't marry her, did I?' he widens his eyes furiously. He is right- everyone knows-but what about his kid? She is the mother of his kid. Dayo looks from face to face, breathing hard, suppressing the tightness in his throat. Should he be there resolving a mindless dispute or still in bed with his wife, yet six hours away, swaddled in a comforting quilt in New York City? To be sincere, he has no say in a knotty union. He wishes Soronje vanished into thin air and allow room for healing. Only a few minutes ago, he just progressed from denial to rage. He thinks she is really loathsome, getting in his way and disrupting his restorative process. So sad, he isn't in position to dismiss her.

'Soronje- so sorry about that. Why not just go for now while I talk to him privately? I need to know what's going on', he stretches his long legs under a glass table, crossed a pair of expensive men's composite high-top sneakers. He looks different: has added weight and even looks fresher than before.

'Thank you so much. I appreciate-', she says with a shaky voice, suffering emotional imbalance. She turns to leave quietly, feels Segun's piercing eyes of contempt on her back. After taking six steps, she remembers why she enters the room, then turns back.

'Segun, can I at least, go out now? You said I mustn't go anywhere today'.

'For all that I care Soronje, you can go to hell. I don't need you for anything around here. Tell me, what should I do with you?', he spreads him arm explicitly. Dayo rolls his eyes, scourged by his inexplicable rant. *Just give a chance to leave-man. Oh God, why is this my business?*

Soronje cranes her neck around at a complete loss. She ponders on refuting him, repaying him in the same coin but remembers Baba's admonition. She storms out of the room like a bubble about to explode. Segun's intent eyes still on her, an insuperable fury building up in him.

'Sorry, Soronje- I'm still around to talk to you. Don't pay attention to his reactions', Dayo says after her, she makes no comment.

'Dayo, let me take you out to a new eatery around. We need to relax somewhere. Oh God, oh my head. We both deserve a break outside this environment'. He walks into his room without waiting for his approval. He knows he wants it, won't deny it.

'Okay', he mumbles, relaxes in the sofa. Now, he is alone. He wraps his hands around his head, stamps his feet and bit his finger in bitter indignation. He knows, without being told, that he has lost it all. He is about to begin his life over again: just like a snake and ladder game. His prospect has ultimately gone down the drain and will certainly never occur to him again. He rose with aggression, kicks the air. *Lord of mercy. Why me? How can I be stupid to neglect him? Why did I leave my client alone? I never did that before.*

In his moment of turbulence, he heard the entrance door opened and closed. He didn't care to peek or check what happens. He is not supposed to be there anyways. He presumes, Soronje leaves with her baby. They are possibly getting away from Segun's threat. That is fair enough, he thinks. What about him? What can he do to walk away from the trouble he returned to? He flinches from the window and walks back into the guest room- his room-to-be.

A gust of dishonor sweeps through him. Better die with honor than live with shame, he thinks. Sooner than he expects, everyone-friends and family will be put in the picture and the rumor will spread like wild fire. He ceases to see his wife and kid, has returned to his way of life.

As he slumps in a sofa beside a new bed, he remembers Labi. She is married to someone, maybe. For a second, he wishes he, at least, said goodbye then switches to his family in America. Life is different for him now. His fear borders on getting his losses back, brushing up and starting over again. It's easier thought out than done but in his creed, courage and conviction outstrip dejection. *In all, I am still thankful for not being caught. Life goes on, no matter the situation. I will not look where I fell but where I slipped. I believe, with my determination; everything will be okay again.*

13

T HE RESONANT TONE OF a Nokia phone pervades the air. Two bars disappear; a winking bar signals relative strength of a low network in the neighborhood. It stops ringing. Segun searches for network from spot to spot and it begins to ring again. With overrated anxiety, he presses the reception button then glues the phone to his ear.

'Hello', his panicky voice filters through to the end, hands trembling like a leaf on a busy lake. Unfortunately, he missed the call. He listens to its disconnecting tone disheartened. His hands drop in devastation as he watches the bars fade away again-one after the other. They're in the middle of nowhere, an eccentric land with esoteric technological encroachment. Civilization ultimately turns its back on them- they remain enemies forever, probably.

His eyes roam around, examining familiarity, something he can acquaint with. Not any occurred to him. Walking fussily, he struggles to pull out his flip-flop from a clammy red earth worsened by a heavy downpour he witnessed on their way. He loses a strap, slows down a bit. He breaks off his pace, to at least, find a cool spot to relax his aching legs and back. It wasn't easy reaching the weird destination.

His grief panned out at an early hour of the day, leaving him in great turbulence. It was a beautiful Saturday. Both friends planned out a well-cooked lunch taken at his patio, talking about friends and past encounters. Not any of them, including Soronje herself, could predict the dismaying turn of event at the crack of dawn. Another three hours passed by and no trace of it till sunset. Segun was awoken by the loudest scream he ever heard in his entire life. Pandemonium broke out. He ran off to his room and saw his ally in an acute lunatic display. He looked straight faced, did not recognize him in any way possible. With the help of a mystified neighbor, he drove at full pelt to the location for spiritual help. Dayo is in trouble.

When his phone begins to ring again, he hurries back to the same spot, spattering mud everywhere, in a rush of anxiety. He doesn't mind- he cares to do what is right at the right time. The phone stops ringing-the network vanishes. He swirled around with a start, vowing never to return there again. It's a sheer waste of time and energy. If he has a chance to return home on time, he plans to call Meghan back.

Segun finally enters the hut, observing his environs. It's all so strange. Tall palm trees sway their fronds lazily over a secluded small hut, festooned with its exact produce and mud. The sun peers, from its rearmost, at some bizarre guests. Black clay pots of all sizes, broken baskets blotched with palm oil, mortars, calabashes and grinding stone take usual position on the ground and squint at the morning sun. The wall is steadfast with its dependents: the broom, pestle, arrow, cutlasses and a large talking drum give as much trust as in the past years they joined the family. A large animal feather akin to peacock fritters away in the air as two flaking lizards scuttle by in a tug of war. Segun remembers his encounters with the village years back. If he hadn't seen the scene himself, he wouldn't believe that crudeness in that form still exists on planet earth. However, what brings him is much more crucial and urgent than a mere distraction from the setting.

He breezes into a room with a bare red- earth floor through a tattered and soiled raffia curtain. A middle-aged woman storms out at the same time, holding a black gourd filled with hazy substance. He hurries back straightaway. He stands a respectable distance away, staring at her, a glaring fear all over him. Not paying attention to him, she utters incantations, invoking spirits, heading towards a nearby forest. *This is wonderful! How did my neighbor discover this kind of place? I respect him from now on.*

Segun shakes his head bewildered. He waits for another two minutes to be called in and no one came. Finally, he makes up his mind to present himself.

Furthest in the large room, he meets the steady gaze of a traditional psychiatrist. He feels his presence, lifts his face silently. Womisan sits on the naked floor pounding herbs and concoction in a small mortar. He lowers his grey hair to carry on, having recognized his face.

'Good morning sir', he looks around for where to sit, turns a deaf ear to his thunderous pounding.

'Take a seat my son', he motions to another mortar turned upside- down, next to him.

'Good morning wise one', he greets again, glaring at a terrifying surrounding, his eyes wandering from item to item. He had no privilege to examine the scene when they first arrived in the morning-when all hell was broken loose. Now he sits next to familiar and strange items on course: a red material embellished with numerous cowries, a pair of dark effigies facing different directions, a horn clothed with feathers, a broken clay pot with splotch of palm oil and salt and a pendulous broom festooned with cowries. Segun sighs heavily then returns his gaze to the busy old man. He is absorbed in his work, mindless of his astute introspection. His infiltrating eyes fall on his feathery-gray hair. Each time he hits the pestle, he screws up his face like one in pain, wielding much more effort than usual. He says nothing to him, won't say something until he talks to him first. Ultimately, to save his time, he speaks to him again.

'How is his health now?' he raises his voice over a noisy clobbering from pestle to mortar. He still doesn't look up at him, he wonders if he heard what he said. But he did.

'Who?'

'Baba- look at me. I brought my friend here this morning- the tall dark and handsome guy', he shot him a belligerent stare. *What kind of elder is this? Can he just look up and save my time? This is important.*

For the first time, he stops pounding and looks straight at him. Segun sees him clearly now. He also looks outlandish like everything he sees there. His eyes are lined black, their prominent redness staring up at him. This is scary, only the one with a lion's heart can behold those grotesque eyes for seconds. His big face is very oily too, they shine like a luminous pot. His face is devoid of hair, no strand on even his brow. And his nostrils are large enough to consume a full moon. From a distance, he watches his gross nasal septum. But he is unique, powerful, bold and intelligent. He keenly awaits his response to learn more about him.

'Dayo?'

'Yes sir, Dayo'.

'That man is in trouble. There are two different women fighting to have him fiercely'. He looks down at the powdery content he made in his mortar and stirs it with the pestle. There are still lumps he has to pulverize before mixing certain herbs he has prepared to relieve a client he got three days ago. He made to continue his work but pauses to conclude with his confounded guest. He watches him flank his mouth open in sheer surprise, the mortar pointed at its target.

'Yes- those women used two incompatible forces on him. They brought him back here against his wish. The propitiation they failed to effect resulted in his trouble'

'They brought him back?', he asked in confusion, his mind affixed on Labi-on getting back here. He curiously asks to discover the other woman. 'Who are these two women?' *Definitely the two women in his life.*

'The oracle says that you know them both. They are the two women in his life'.

'Ahn- now I see', he widens his eyes in full awareness. Labi and Meghan, definitely. He peers around in confusion. How could Meghan possibly know about voodoo if she never lived in Africa? As for Labi, he knew she wouldn't have given up easily with all she's been through. She only visits his apartment to supervise her handiwork, perhaps. He bent his arms on his thighs, leans forward in his seat in deep thought, his brow creased, eyes dark with rage. *What have men done to these women to deserve this kind of punishment? Can love be original? Can I love naturally? Why must the worst and most terrible in character impose herself on me? Why? What can we do to save our heads from this trouble? What? Soronje tied me down, now my friend faces the risk of being deranged forever. Why are we always victims of love?*

'Your friend put himself in this trouble. He is too greedy. If you know you don't want to marry a woman, leave her alone. Let her be. Deception is bad', Womisan breaks in his memory, his enormous lips wrapping back and forth in a guileless discussion. He is right-he knows he is, but he isn't disposed to declare that at the moment. Whoever falls in a ditch teaches others to follow a different path. Dayo's situation has taught him faithfulness in a relationship. Whatever you won't eat, don't smell. However, the solution is more registered on his mind.

'Baba Womisan, please sir, help me cure him. He is my close brother; I don't want anything bad to happen to him. Madness is a shame-a total disgrace. Right now, I haven't informed his family because he came home and-'

'I see everything here. I have seen all with my third eye', he cuts him short.

'You see what I mean?', he looks at his forehead closely for the third eye and acknowledges its invisible.

'I will cure him, but he will still be in trouble. He is in a critical situation'.

'What danger again?'

'One after the other. Let's cure this madness first'. Leaving Segun in his silent thought, he shoves the mortar forward, makes to rise to his feet. It appears he forgot something. He stretches his legs, trying to plan his work out proportionately. In his wards, he has fifteen clients he must cure before the end of the year, each having different conditions. While some are self-imposed challenges, others are from friends and families who wish to turn back the hands of time or meet out a punishment. To him, humans are wicked.

'Kekere! Kekere!!', Womisan shouts, preparing to get up and find his little apprentice. He draws the mortar closer, tosses some herbs in it and waits for him to surface.

'Give me that bag', he asks Segun who now feels at sea. He follows his direction and clutches a small knitted bag hanging with a number of eccentric sacks on the wall.

As he opens his mouth to ask an important question, Kekere enters the room hurriedly. He is a short and robust man in his early thirties. He wears a pair of immeasurably dirty shorts, holding a whip in his hand, his spiky hair and face as his master's.

'Kekere, take this man to our new patient'.

'Yes sir. Fijabi poured his concoction away. I gave him five strokes of my whip for that. You know it took you five days to prepare that thing he trampled on', he feeds a pot back to him. Segun watches mysteriously. He shakes his head in sympathy for his dear friend. Only God knows when he will be in good health - free from every conflict.

'Leave him alone. He will remain here till next year if he allows the evil in him to ruin his recovery. Please take this gentleman to the new patient. We have more works to do today', he starts his pounding again, not waiting for a response from either of them. Kekere takes the lead, moving fast and furious, his buttocks in a free fleet swing. Segun turns away irritably. Nothing about the short young man interests him; he seems not to care about his carriage.

When they arrived, he bursts into a ward and descends on a brawny man chained to a metal pole. He lashes out at him ceaselessly. Segun holds his hands the sixth time he takes it up.

'That's okay. What did he do?', he looks straight at him. Is he only showing off to him or reveling in pleasure of being the one in control? It is quite unfair.

'This man is not ashamed of himself. Every time, he will do this nonsense', he explains breathlessly, his eyes fixed on him, his predisposition pushing him to hit him more. His client laughs hard at him, rolls on the floor, insensible of the phenomenon, his dilemma getting the best of him.

In Segun's mind, he pictures what more will befall his friend in a tense situation as such. He keeps falling from grass to grass. Obviously, he will be mistreated like the other patients he sees there. Despite their involvement with the traditional psychiatrist, he believes and prays for God's intervention.

'Where is my portfolio, give me my portfolio!', another client shrieks from a different ward.

'He doesn't know what he is saying or doing. You can't judge him by his actions right now. Please take me to my friend'. He hands his whip back to him, steps aside for him to lead the way. Looking straight in the direction his ally laid half lost to the world, he sighs heavily. Kekere deciphers his reaction, frowns at his intrusion, disgruntled at his suspended obsession. It's how he avenges those that would have oppressed or suppressed him in the society, those that would look down on him and take advantage of his look. The ones that wouldn't have respected him if not for their situation. As nature would have it, he stepped out of his low self-esteem and tries to even the score. No one can stop him, even a defender's friend is an object.

'I'm returning to give you the portfolio. You will get your portfolio today. I will be right back', he storms off the spot enraged. Segun follows, questioning his psychosis. The unresolved mystery of integrating spanking with client's treatment bothers his mind. But for the exigency stimulating their arrival, he thinks it isn't the right option. If he is going to be through all that, then life is unfair-unfair to take his friend up and slope him to the mat of dishonor. When he recollects how he made it to the top in just a while and skidded back unexpectedly, he shakes his head in sheer pity. He gives in to his emotion and sheds a little tears.

In another section of the hut, on a bare floor and surrounding dilapidated walls, Dayo is tied down to a metal pole alongside two other new clients. He looks weird: hair ruffled, eyes distraught and teeth gnashing and half- opened like a wild dog ready to bark and attack. Segun looks shocked. It's surprising how he suddenly transformed into that scary being in only a few hours. What happens in the next thirty days is unpredictable. At the moment, he learnt to believe in the psychiatrist's prescriptions. Besides, he still trusts and believes that with God, all things are possible.

Dayo doesn't recognize him. He sizes him up from head to toe at first then bursts out laughing. He sees an intruder invading his home in New York. He snatches his watch, and escapes through his basement exit. He looks at him closely, still reasoning backward and in profound absurdity. He makes to strike at him. Seeing his behavioral changes, Segun takes a couple of steps backward, praying inwardly. His friend is insane, absolutely out of the world and he doesn't identify anyone again.

'Dayo- it's me, your friend. Dayo, look at my face. it's me, Segun', taking two cautious steps, he approaches carefully. His eyes fall on a freshly sustained injury on his knotted wrists- then a conjoined rope to his ankle. *Oh God! Have mercy! Show your mercy, this is unbearable.* Still in his sky-blue jeans, and a black shirt, he looks handsome but not at peace. He sits and stares straight at him, dancing to the whims of life, suffering from his illusory past. Torrent of shame lashes him to the marrow, his head controlled by the unseen, his directions misunderstood by his atmosphere. As he watches him on a bare floor, in the filth, all certainties vanish and the distress he felt the previous night resumes. He struggles to regain consciousness to no avail. Film of tears form in his Segun's eyes. He welcomes his wishful thought with tears in his eyes. *Can a magic quickly restore his sanity? Is it possible he is healed on the spur of the moment and they have to return home together? Can they be back to his cozy apartment and begin the next day in a party mood? And plan a new life or discuss pending issues? Can the curse be removed, and he will never be there again?* Not again, in his entire life.

'He will be fine in the next two years-in two years he will get well', Kekere reassures him. Segun flashes him an angry stare, sizes him from his dusty feet. *Oh God, this guy is ugly and mean! Years!* Did he just say years? To be candid, he was being sincere to him. Their medicine is a long-term healing process. Some clients have been there for about six years.

Dayo suddenly bursts into a jolting laughter. He laughs harder and harder. Kekere advances to shut him up, his usual way but for the presence of his friend. He drops his hands wearily, prepares to show him to the door. Really, he is disturbing his work, no one gives their client a special treatment. They are all treated equally.

'When are you coming back to check on him?', he walks out of the room, leading the way to the exit. He waits impatiently to gain his attention, nevertheless, he isn't ready to go.

'Tomorrow. I will bring someone to stay with him', he wipes the tears in his eyes, standing and staring down at him.

'Stay with him? We don't do that here. We will take care of him, you don't have to do that', he frowns at his proposition. Of all the clients there, there isn't someone with anyone. Why is he different? He scratches his head to bring up a fresh issue that will prompt his leave. The way he stands and behold him is strange. He looks like he would get inside of him and operate whatever disrupts his mind, but it doesn't work that way. Patience and trust is the key.

Finally, he walks out of the room quietly and he follows him to the exit. This time, he doesn't look back, only proceeds to his car, where his neighbor awaits his good news. He hears Kekere faring him well faintly but wasn't listening. His mind is far away. First to the women that wreck him that bad and the aftermath of his support to unburden him. Where does he proceed from here?

14

IT's A COOL SATURDAY morning in the month of July. The atmosphere turns clammy, clouds over progressively in a mass of condensed liquid, floating in the sky. In no time, daytime envelopes in humidity and metamorphoses into dark, humid forged nighttime. Silvery forks of lightning illumines the sky, aggravating a howling thunder. There comes the slenderest chance to run and canopy before the downpour of a chilly rain- in showers and putters. It rains cats and dogs. In thirty-two minutes, it is over. With its obvious scuds darting across and, betokening a cool day, the azure sky is a stunning spectacle. Birds chirp from tree to tree, singing praises in the quietness of a pleasant day on Johnson street. A hawk soars singly while a group of little birds hover with a crucial group.

Around the sequestered and sparsely peopled street are stunning structures and tall gates. All entries are firmly shut to forestall invasion visiting in the day. The street itself is a dead end with the biggest gate for safety.

Segun drives in slowly, pondering on perfecting his mission. Now, that they hold a whip hand over him, he needs to be careful. Numbly, he leans backward in his seat, in deep thought. He regains control of his emotion when the car jolts to a halt at his destination. For five minutes, he holds the steering, still at the same spot, predicting the outcome of the news he is about to sniff out. He finds himself on the horns of dilemma: disclosing the information or sleeping on it till his friend recovers. *I have to inform them. I can't handle this alone. I am really scared of the consequences.* He closes his eyes depressed. He gets more desirous of a grim determination that strengthens him and possibly breaks him free from a burdensome ordeal. When he opens his eyes, they are blood shot, pregnant with anxiety. He feels panicky. A thought crosses his mind and he wants to reverse and just back off while a sturdier conviction emerges to support his persistence. *It's time to open up.* It rings on and on. He storms out of the car, full of impulsive gestures, slams the door and pulls himself together.

He proceeds toward a white gate, numbered house 25. His taps occur light but audible. He steps aside for appearance. In less than two minutes, he hears flip flop clapping and progressing towards the gate.

'Good morning', he greets, straining his eyes to observe the attendant through a fissure beside the gate.

'Brother Segun. It's quite a long time- this is incredible. Are you really the one here? Quite ages since we saw you', Teju unlocks the gate, almost impatiently. Just that morning, she was complaining to her mum about her brother. In a long time, they haven't heard from him. Could anything be wrong with him or he simply took on the immigrant's way of blanking out their nationalities? Whatever the situation may be, she is relieved, Segun is there.

'Not the case. I've been too occupied with work. You know? I have to go to the office in the morning and arrive late at night. It isn't easy around here, sis', he smiles, watching her throw the gate open. He walks through and steps aside for her to finish up.

She looks around curious, watches his car for a moment then rather asks, 'you don't want to drive in your car?'

'No, I think it's okay right there', he looks back at the mansion behind him, gathers a long sigh, then returns his gaze to Teju, Dayo's only sister and sibling.

Her seraphic face arrests his attention. At twenty-four, she holds the best carriage he ever saw. And being the only daughter of the Ogundare's, she is turned off iniquity by their disciplined parents. She isn't given much opportunities to relate with friends or exposed to social life at all. All schedules are usually from home to school or home to stores. No time hanging out with friends for the fear of peer influence and corruption. Dayo was almost trained up the same way but being a male, he earned his freedom earlier in high school.

'Do you have a message from my brother? I know something very important must have brought you here', she looks into his eyes, searchingly, has missed him so much.

'Yes- there is a good news from him', he gives a masked pretense, drives a smile.

'Good news? Okay, tell me first. What is it?', she holds his hands, looks up at him smiling.

'Let me see your daddy first then I will get back to you', he cuts the jokes short, wears a resolute expression. He isn't there to play. Seeing this, she frees his hand and steps back to lock the gate in a hurry. He says nothing more, only walks in their large living room to find Mr. Ogundare.

Segun meets him sitting in a homely sofa. He stretches

his legs on a table and reads from a tabloid, his bespectacled eyes skidding off a fresh page. He lowers the tabloid to have a full view of his visitor.

'Segun? Is this you?', he takes off his spectacles and rubs his palm over his face.

'Good morning sir', he bows to him courteously, a flippant smirk playing around his lips.

'What happened? You stopped visiting since your friend travelled ', he slaps the paper on a large brown table, drops his legs with care. Over the years, he changes gradually. He looks different from the zestful man he used to know. Age has fostered him into a prudent, less ferocious man.

'We don't see you here again. Is it because your friend is not around?' he forgets to offer him a seat.

'No, its work. I-', he looks around then smiles wryly.

He knows how to take a seat and make himself comfortable as usual but what brings him there is exigent. It stands him up, bows his head. Its better discussed standing and wrapping his arms behind him.

'Do you hear from your friend? We haven't heard from him in a long time'.

'That's why I'm here', finally, he sits down, at the edge of the closest sofa to him. He begins his narration, first with parables and proverbs, then swifts from one related issue to the other, and point to point. The elderly looks at him bewildered, trying to make a sense out of his demonstrations. Finally, he breaks the news.

'What?! You mean he is back in your apartment?', he leans forward, his eyes widening in great shock.

'Y-yes sir. He got back and-'.

'Did he send you to inform me about this or what? Why

Eniola. F. Fagbemi

didn't he come here?', he looks aggressive, searches his face
for a quick answer. He looks worried, confused.

'Yes sir, there is a situation'. He sighs and bites his
finger. Again, he regrets accepting him in his apartment.
He contemplates giving the other information, seeing
his first reaction. If he sounded that way on the first one,
successive reaction on the bad news would possibly be
bad. That would be it for the day. He would tell him, he
returned to him, then left his apartment to live elsewhere-
somewhere he doesn't know. Just then, an impulse begins
to probe the essence of his visit. If that's the reason he goes
there, then what is the need? He chooses to keep another
secret after all.

'So- why is he not here with you?'

'He left. He left my apartment two weeks ago and-' he
smartly thinks of a better conclusion to craft his lies. 'I'm
here to check if he returns home or-'

'Or what? He's not here. No one has seen him, and you
must call him out for us. You saw him, didn't you?'

'Yes'.

Before he says another word, he rises from his seat, his
enormous height dwarfing his tormented body on the sofa.
Segun also rises along to preclude an attack.

'Listen, young man! I think my son has been acting
on your advice. You tell him what to do. You told him
not to return home and you know where he is. God, I
thank you for pushing this man here to acknowledge his
sin,' he raises his face to the ceiling, talks to his illusory
creator, then returns his gaze to his waiting offender. He
looks confounded, sizing him up for the first time since he
knew him as his nostalgic father. *Did he harbor some sort of*

hatred for me before? Why is he overreacting? Doesn't he trust me anymore? He knew me since I was a child. He stands akimbo, prepares to defend himself. He knew it will lead to this, but he won't open his eyes and get himself into trouble. He maintains his stance.

'No sir. I don't know where he is. I also came here to find him'.

'Look at me young man. I give you only twenty-four hours to call him out for me, else-', he raises a warning finger at him then walks off, leaving him standing in the middle of the living room. He had barely entered when he made his way out of the house. He finds the gate partly allied to its large metal lock. And in the next five minutes, he is on his way home.

Its drizzling, the climate is getting cold- a cloudy atmosphere promises a fresh start of another heavy downpour. His windscreen wiper busily take off droplets of rain from his view in slow progression. In almost two miles, they get in a race as heavy rain splish-splashes, trample in his view. Segun sighs. *What is the need to suffer this much? To reap trouble and regret? If I knew he will have a problem, I wouldn't have helped him. How do I deny my confession now? I should have kept my mouth shut till he recovers. Oh God, help me.*

15

'**H**ONEY, DID YOU ASK the psychiatrist the cause of your friend's sickness?', Soronje asks looking at her husband seriously. After the unfortunate circumstance, he hasn't had time to put his feet up or get around to divulge the heart of the matter. Even after she dropped in on Baba and paid for his fortification later on the same day, she still visualizes the ordeal visiting his life, convinced by his prophecy. All the same, she wants to connect with him in a way, to discreetly detect his acquaintance of her involvement in their sinful acts. Or rebuff being involved at all.

'Soronje, can you spare me? I don't feel like talking to anyone. I just want to be alone right now, so- please- go', he takes three drained steps away from her. He has too much on his mind to resolve, particularly the Ogundare's hassle he dug out for himself.

'Don't you think that someone may be responsible for his problem? Maybe a woman', she persists, following him to his room closely. For her disclosure, he sneaks a look at her, grows wildly suspicious of her. Even though he isn't prepared for her loose tongue, he gives a chance to listen to her. Who knows? She may be wisely foolish this time.

'What do you mean by that?', he asks without interest.

'You may not know why I'm asking this question.', she takes a passing interest in the matter, being meddlesome and giving signals that she is bound up in trouble.

'You may not know', she adds, 'but I will reserve my comment if you don't want to hear'. She looks away sadly. Her instinct propels her further, stimulates her to spit out a burning secret at the edge of eruption. She must deliver it or remain twitchy around him.

'Soronje, I am very tired. If you have anything to say, please say and leave me alone', he rolls his eyes objectionably, needed to alleviate the strain on his lids and of course her spontaneous disruption. He thinks he has suffered far too much of tossing and turning since the past three days-he hasn't had time to relax. Now that she is there, he isn't prepared to argue.

'And that your restlessness is really bothering me. I mean, I can't watch you suffer for what you know nothing about', she presses on.

'Soronje, please- please, I plead with you to just say what you have to say and leave me alone', he closes his eyes, still in demonstration of his vile mood. *I don't care to hear whatever you have to say anyways.* He made to close his room door, but she pushes and lunges through to proceeds after him. He sinks in his bed, holds his head and cries within for rescue from the devil in his life. His belly is crowded with disagreeable talks and revelations about all her treacheries in his existence. He withholds for protection. His life is at stake if he disdains her at the moment. Whether he likes it or not, he is fiercely hers forever. *Possible impossibilities.* Yes, he can stomach that, tolerate her but he needs his space.

'Do you know that Labi is responsible for his problem?' she says finally, flaring her eyes in all seriousness. Segun's jaw drops in surprise, hearing the same exposure from her. Obviously, she knows something about it. He gives the hardest, most spiteful look she ever got since he got tired of her. *Is she a witch?* As if reading his mind, it isn't long before she gives a response.

'Yes- are you surprised? She said she will do it because he followed another woman to America. Labi is very wicked'. Segun watches her with profound amazement, his tiredness disappearing.

'She told me about it. I discouraged her but she didn't listen', she raises her voice, seeing him lend an ear. First, he had no interest, now he wants her to spill all the beans, say everything she knows about the plot.

'Really? What about the madness?', he raises his hand to control her noise. Understanding all his nonverbal gestures, she obeys. She continues, struggling with an unusual low tone.

'What madness? That girl is very dangerous. She told me that she was warned not to return him home, but she refused. That madness is the consequence of her spell'. She sees the expression on his face and turns away disappointed. She has lived with him for four years now, doesn't need someone to express how he feels at different times. His cheerless eyes are beset by unseasonable discovery of distrust and misery. She is guilted into welcoming a sense of betrayal. He thinks the poor helpless lady, perchance accepted her devilish ploy as a confidant and now, the opposite is inevitable.

For a while, he views her with intermittent sigh of

exasperation. He knows precisely all she did to hold him in the relationship and make him have a change of heart. He never had a plan to marry her when all is said and done but all at once, she was accepted as the mother of his child. He knows all about that. Coupled with her recent confession, he calculates, it's time to quit their relationship once and for good.

'Soronje, look at me closely. I am done with you', his face clouds up. He feels the urge to beat her up, however his principles predominate his thoughts. He clenches his fists, break them with measured process. He shudders with rage, paces around the room.

'What is wrong with you? Have you been infected by your friend?', she looks bewildered.

'I am done with you! Be gone before I return to this house'.

He can't sleep as planned anymore. He rushes to get his shirt and trousers. Not looking up at her, or her four-year-old daughter that stumbles on him on the threshold, he rushes in his trousers. Bolanle looks from mum to dad and dad to mum. She has seen them fight almost all the time, throw shade at each other before her eyes and even teach her to speak inappropriate words. They are a great match of errors in her life. Segun gave every consideration to remain in the illicit marriage for her sake but now, it won't work anymore. He still wants to play his fatherly role in her life, only with the absence of Soronje in his life.

'Daddy-', she calls after him as he slams the door. He may be very sorry for his acts later; not at the time he is furious about an impending invasion of his destiny. Soronje twisted the hands of fate, now he twists their future.

By the time he is gone, and she stands facing her

innocent kid, she doubts his unanticipated decision. That should be a prank, peradventure. *Segun, you are fiercely mine forever. You are going nowhere! Baba is still alive, you go nowhere. As long as he lives, you are going nowhere!*

She also rushes in her room to prepare a visit to the shrine that entwines their future. Has it lost its control? She must visit right away. Again, Bola gets in her way and she is propelled towards her room where she also prepares to spend time with her grandma. Her lips are pursed- her face wraps up in unwary mood. Young as she is, she begins to wonder why she always has to be the one in the middle whenever situations occur. In her little mind, she dwells in unformed plausibility. *Why do they always have to fight? Why do the adults fight too? Oh my God! She won't have my time again. This isn't good for me. Why is my daddy angry with me? But I did nothing. I wish he said something.*

16

O N A TUESDAY MORNING, in the month of August, Kekere breezes out of their consulting room, carrying a big black pot of concoction, chin raised, chest protruded, vigor fabricated in pain. At the entrance, he gently sits it on the floor and peers around for the little calabashes he uses to serve his clients. His eyes rest upon their different locations, their faces mostly turned down. That isn't difficult as long as he still holds his control. Nothing fascinates him like the moment he exercises the power conferred on him to push, flog, order and attack the dignity of his numerous victims. Failure to submit triggers malevolence. He smiles, fetching a calabash. A swarm of flies buzz away when he reaches for the third one. All calabashes laid there unwashed for a whole day. Following their routine morning hygiene, he is obligated to clean them all before proceeding to serve the clients. But he is indubitably exhausted, can't guarantee a reserved energy to accomplish the task. A new client was muscled in the previous day by a group of men. He appeared the most ferocious and burliest client he encountered this year. Since the first time he saw him, he measures to a broad-shouldered cardboard fighter, thick bulging biceps like a log of twisted wood, enormous arms and great height. Is he a wrestler? He presumes he is one thing or another before he was admitted. His appearance led him into trouble, maybe.

He was awoken in the early hour of the next day with punctual punches from the same new man. He had set himself free, ripping off all the rope that shackled him to a pole. When it was time to get even with his assailants, he made for him. Now, he feels like a vertebra is broken in his neck. He's been having a stinging sensation around his neck and chest all the time. He stoops to fill the calabashes one after another. With perfection, he clips three calabashes with two fingers, another nestling in his second hand. He has one more lying on the floor. He would return for that, right after going round the wards and start over again from the next ward.

He proudly grasps his whip and continues towards the seventh room, where Rondo sits on a mat, turning his eyes in every direction like a new bride, bursting into unrestrained laughter from time to time. Only he is responding to treatment after his long stay in the ward. Five years ago, he was brought to them by force of circumstances. His illness, according to his rescuer, began after he laid false charges against his best friend. Within the first three years, it was a fate worse than death. He was stark raving mad, barking and tearing at his skin. *So terrible.* During the third and fourth year, he kept mute while the fifth year marked the beginning of his recovery. Now, he asks after everyone amidst a dubious smile that brightens his once haunted face.

'Drop it and leave! Dirty man', he kicks Kekere's leg and for a reason, the pain travels to his throbbing neck. He turns and whips him on his loin. Today, he is aggrieved. He won't let anyone cross him up. He walks out on him, slams the door shut.

The fifth door welcomes him with its usual firmness. He pushes at it, still holding the concoction. He is propelled to the front. His second shot was successful. The wooden door succumbs to his attack and falls inexorably to the edge of the room, a loud cracking sound fills the air. Labi rises up with a start, struggles to flip a wrapper around her nudity. Kekere hurries to cover his face with both hands, still leaving a little but discernible space between to glimpse at her stunning body.

'Are you crazy? Are you insane? What do you think you are doing?'', she pulls a blouse down her body in a jiffy.

'What do you mean? What have I done wrong? This is not your room, remember?', he spreads his arms, a little concoction spilling on the floor. They both look down at a round dampness forming on the spot. Who cares about what comes from the little man? She hates him to the moon back, and wishes he never existed there. Does he like her too? No, he thinks she is too pompous. He wishes she wasn't there for his client. This is the fourth time they will disagree after he met her.

'Please, let me do my job. I am here to serve my client not you!'

'Give me that thing and get away from here!', she snatches the calabash from him, a whole lot of its content spilling everywhere. She hisses, drops it aside and shows him to the door, 'leave!'

Kekere slows down a little bit, looks straight at her. What is she trying to do? Take on his position? There s no way that will work as long as he exists. The best solution would be dismissing her with his client. He draws a long sigh, then storms out of the room, breathing hard.

Labi sighs as she yanks the door close behind him. What a sweet sorrow. She walks off the spot like a disconsolate widow, the calabash in her hand. She peers around confused, then drops it beside their mat. Once more, she pull a long breath of sorrow.

The event of her grief seems like a bad dream – unutterable misadventure occurring in rapid succession. And who shoulders all the guilt? Dayo, who elopes with a woman and forgot she ever existed in his life? Or Soronje who attaches verisimilitude to the odd charm that generates more glitches in their lives? Or even Labi herself for her impatience and failure to hunt up a gratifying clarification? No, could it ever be the loneliness she found difficult to strike back at after his departure? Or sheer jealousy sniffing at her face? One of these reasons patently has a devastating effect on their situation.

She makes a sharp turn towards her beloved in his moment of rest, his head pillowed on his arm. Her penetrating eyes travel from his gorgeous face to his hairy chest, down to his toes and back to his face. He sleeps in peace, sleeps away his destiny in America. Is she righteous at all? What happens to all the unfailing sermons in her church and her true confession in the presence of God? Are they practicable in any way possible? She slumps to the ground, holding her head in her hands. For the pain she caused the young man, she wallows in self-blame, hopes she never knew Soronje.

She hears mumbles and lifts her face to him, tears

filling her eyes. *Thank God for the pills, sleep would have eluded him forever. He wouldn't even have remembered what it means to sleep. Why would I do that? Why should I inflict pain on him and usher distress in his life? Is this for love? No, its not worth the pain and setback.*

She rubs her face with the back of her hand and stares at him amorously. He is heavily possessed but still remains her heart's desire. Deep within her, she has that unchallenging urge to win him back from the spirits dominating his life: a sorely difficult dream that may never come true. From positivity, her mind dawdles to the realm of impossibilities. She begins to question her stance in that scenario. What would be her fate if eventually, there isn't a solution to the problem? And he stays unsound forever. She would have to spend the rest of her life with him, even though he is off his chump. *God almighty! Why me? Why us? Do we deserve this? I want him back. I know, you made it possible for me to bring him back, but I can't marry him in this situation. God, please, make a way. You are the Alpha and Omega. Make a way.*

Sadly, she sits beside him and stretches her long, elegant legs. Her spirit sinks at the prospect of the trouble yet uncovered from his sordid past. Baba had earlier warned that he would jump from frying pan to fire. The driving force of his untrue love gives him more trouble-he is sincerely in a serious trouble. He is at a loss what is happening to him presently but what happens after he cuts loose from the predicament.

'Labi', Dayo breaks into her thought.

'Hmm-?', she swirls around to meet his steady gaze, her face full of surprise.

'How are you?', he leans on the wall, arms between his legs.

'I'm fine- I'm fine. Dayo, you're recovering. You recognize me'. She rushes to him happily. Since he started receiving his treatment, he has not been able to correctly identify anyone around him, not even his bosom friend who he could figure out in the dark.

'Where are we?', he looks around him.

'Dayo-you've been sick ', she explains. A flicker of smile crosses her lightened face, her thumbs brushes his brows fondly.

'Sick? Sick? Sick? Okay? It's you Edward. I just completed the task. Can I do something else for you? Okey-dokey, I'm gonna take my leave right now! I'm done for the day. Have a good one'. He goes over the last statement in rapid succession, smiling.

'Dayo!', she hisses. 'Look', she continues with a feeling of apprehension, 'are you happy I'm sick at heart? Was it not you that spoke to me just now? Can you please control yourself? Look at me, I can't go to school because of you', she bursts into tears.

'Oh baby is crying', he laughs crazily.

Now out of spirit, she gives him a respectable distance, crying her eyes out. *What you truly love, you cannot ignore, and the product of love are faith and hope. But I am afraid. Will he continue like this? Is there a solution? Obviously, none at this time. Oh God, I shouldn't have listened to Soronje.*

'Hello, good morning', Segun's voice surfaces from the back of the door. 'It seems they are asleep', he refers to his companion.

'Good morning' he calls again. Labi swiftly unties her

wrapper, squeezes into a pair of jeans. She wonders why Segun visits again. He earlier informed that he wouldn't be there due to his trip to a neighboring state. What brought him back is mysterious.

'Yes, come in- brother Segun. We are not sleeping; the door is opened. It isn't locked. Come in', she wipes the tears in her eyes, cocks an eye at Dayo. He lowers his head in deep thought, quivering.

'You can come in', Segun holds the bamboo door for Meghan. She darts an impatient look at the place the instant she enters.

'Is this the place?', she says in American accent. Behind a modishly tinted pair of glasses, her eyes fall on Labi's face, dilly-dallies along her slim but shapely physique then makes a quick-witted turn towards Dayo. He still lowers his head like a mat weaver. She holds her gaze for a moment then asks, 'Dayo, what happened to you?' When he gives no response, she retorts, 'are you also deaf and dump?', she takes a few steps backward, pondering the nature of his sickness. Her sense of misgiving sets in.

'He talks. He is neither deaf nor dumb', Segun corrects her undesirable insinuation.

'Honey, we have to return to America. You have no business here. And are they aware that you are married now? Where is his wedding ring?', she sizes him up, looks at Labi spitefully. The message is for her, clear or unclear. They are married.

'I didn't see him with any ring'. Segun looks around blankly. In all sincerity, he never returned with a ring. He pulled it before his arrival. Segun is at a loss what to do now, since he vowed not to relate to Labi about him. He merely took her to the scene to look after him and help hasten his recovery process. After all, she is the driving force behind his ordeal. The situation pushes him to ask imperative questions, only from her. She could assist to clear all doubts on the ring. Who knows if she has it?

'I don't know what you're talking about', she forms an opinion of his nature. He is, indeed, a monkey in the middle. Knowing the relationship between them, is he in position to question her about a ring? Before, she gets over the shock, he asks again.

'Can you ask him for us, since you take care of him?'

To this, she gives no answer, only rises to engage in a chore. Before their arrival, she wanted to clean up the room. And their presence seems not to bother her, since they have nothing serious to say. Meghan's eyes follow her everywhere she goes. She doesn't care after she fought and subjugated the thief snatching a beloved from her years ago. She relaxes and enjoys karma whilst it lasts. This is the only time she feels no remorse whatsoever.

'Chickens! What are chickens doing here? Eew, they are so messy. Bad chickens. Shoo'. Dayo shoots his mouth at Segun and Meghan, kicks off a fresh lunatic display, smiling.

While she leans over to fold his shirts she washed earlier that day, she peeks at Meghan's outfit. She wears a yellow shirt over a pair of blue jeans. Her clothes look gorgeous, but she doesn't look as pretty as she imagined. *What a shame! Is this why he left me? She's not worth it anyways*. Not the kind of woman she can rub elbows with in attraction. She merely used her influence to snatch what is hers. God so good, he is back. *Foolish woman. You don't know that your willingness to receive love determines your ability to sow love. You can't just come and take him away from me like that. What I have sown, you cannot reap! I will reap the fruits of my labor.*

'Who is this lady? And you- enough of that mockery, if you want to break free!', Meghan points a finger at them rudely. Segun sighs. She is being difficult. Is she there to fight or solve his problem?

'Oh, I'm sorry, she is his caregiver', Segun introduces with diligence. He knows the effect of breaking legal rules. No relationship outside legal marriage to avert a jail term. Labi flashes him a disappointing stare then returns to her work, still ignoring the trouble she just met. She reserves all her remarks till she leaves the room.

'Excuse me, what was that about? Why do you have to hire his ex as his caregiver.' At this, Segun is shocked. Did she know her before? He prepares his mind for his next response, Labi gets tired of her steadfastness. She drops the shirt in her grasp, straightens to look straight at her.

'You are surprised, right? Are you? Don't be surprised. Dayo told me everything, even showed me your pictures, so I know you so well. He is my husband, stop fooling yourselves here'. She folds her arms across her chest gallantly, casts a demanding stare at her. Labi holds her gaze too. Segun feels like they are being controlled by her. What more does she want after all the supports they have given him?

Labi begins to pace around the room. She feels a sudden heat from within, can't take it anymore. Segun observes this and gestures to her to remain calm.

'The truth is, I am not comfortable with her around my hubby. Can you hire somebody else for me?', she yells rudely. Segun pulls back, his serenity running out of potency. Who does she think she is? He does all things for Dayo, not her. Besides, the only one that cares for him is Labi and that's why she's there. Sooner, he's prepared to see who lives with him in that situation.

Labi drops the pants in her hands, opens the door and takes her leave, tired of her war of words. If that's what Dayo brought upon himself, he should deal with it.

'Labi-Labi, come back, Segun calls her to no avail. Without warning, Dayo also rises up at the same time, made a lunge for the door.

'What?!', Segun places a restraining hand on him, an element of surprise registered on his face.

'What's going on here? Has he been pretending?', Meghan gasps in astonishment.

'No- leave me alone, my soul mate is going. Let me follow her', he struggles with Segun.

'Dayo, look at your wife! Your wife is here'.

'Shhsh. What wife are you talking about? What a shame? You know he has a wife and you still brought in his ex! Seriously? I am disappointed in you', Meghan rants on. Right now, he can't possibly pursue two troubles at the same time. He disregards Meghan and battles against his friend's crisis.

'Dayo, sit down now! Be seated. Don't go nowhere'.

Ruefully, he rebuffs his seemingly convoluted explanations and resumes his position on the mat. His newly developed attitude, and unspeakable rudeness are all products of memory disorder and mental illness that everyone finds difficult to control. This is quite overwhelming but his timely reaction to circumstances makes matters inconceivable. Also, it's an indication that he is on the road to recovery, although not permanent. Things are beginning to look up, if only Meghan relaxes.

For a couple of minutes, she is short of words. She stands marveling at what she just saw.

'Dayo, I know you've been faking. Yes, you are pretending', she blinks, an aura of betrayal all around her.

'No- remember he lost his mind. He doesn't know what he's doing', Segun pleads on his behalf.

'When you are out of here, I'm gonna divorce you. You liar, cheat'.

'Meghan, em- er, please wait', Segun rushes after her.

'Hey- hey, why are rushing after a raccoon? Look at a damsel, she is a damsel,' he laughs and blinks in reminiscence of something. He pauses and looks around. He made a lunge for the door again, feeling a surge of desire for a broken love. He regains his memory a little bit- his curious eyes fall on his clothes, then his surrounding. *Where am I? Why am I alone here? Where is Segun, my dearest friend? And Meghan, my helper? I just met Labi again. Wasn't she here? No one is here. Am I kidnapped? Where is this place? I have to leave right now. Right now!* And this time, he is free to go.

17

'**Y**OU VISITED MY HOUSE to inform us that you friend is with you, didn't you?', Mr. Ogundare anticipates a constructive response, looking at his suspect like a thief awaiting trial. At this point, he's enormously angered by his inconsistency, each day visiting with no answers to lingering questions. His recurrently disallowed calls and aloofness force the crying need to be there bright and early and talk eyeball to eyeball. He can still remember, quite alright, his information. To his utmost surprise, he tells a different story now.

'Darling, leave him alone. By the time we hand him over to the police, he will tell the truth. I'm very sure he used him for rituals', Mrs. Ogundare chips in, folding up her sleeve, stamping her feet in vile display of her anxiety. Since he related the sad message on the same day he dropped in on them, she has been displeased. She longed for a time to find him and clear all doubts.

'Oh no- mummy, don't accuse me of his afflictions. I have no hands in it. I only helped him as a friend'. Segun rises to open his windows. In only five seconds, they both fling open, his whole being engulfed in a passionate anger.

The situation will always get out of control if his parents mistrust him that much.

'And do you think we will ever believe you?', Mr. Ogundare gives a sigh of distress, walking up to him overtly. Segun fixes his glance on the ceiling, deliberates on what to say to persuade them to believe him.

'Segun, you are also my son. In fact, you have been a good son. But- I don't know why you don't want me to see your friend. You know how important he is to me', he draws a long breath and adds, 'he is my only son'. He drops his hands and walks back to his seat, folding his hands behind him disconsolately. Now, Segun is confused. Many gloomy thoughts fill his mind: the same sensation he had when he announced the sad news. How will they comprehend him when he announces that, shortly after the visit, all things turned around. He absconds from where he gets his treatment and has not been found since then. How can he explain this? How will he make them believe that? Won't they conclude that he lied to carry out his bad plan on him? Or even conclude that he used him for money rituals. This trouble will not involve only his helper but also Womisan, who did not know when he sneaked out of the hut. None has happened to him since his thirty years of practice. All these are account to settle but overall, he shoulders the blame for being their informant.

He walks off the spot and sits on a sofa closer to flat screen television. From the blank screen, he watches their reflection. Mr. Ogundare coils in his seat, squinting at him eagerly; his wife looks thunderous. To him, the situation would have been easy as a pie if Mr. Ogundare visited alone. He would have arranged people to find him in Waranshesa. But his wife's presence seems to turn the issue up and down. She will always set his face against every vindication.

'Segun, if you like, turn your face away from me. And keep waiting for us to say good bye to you. You must take us to Dayo before we leave here', she changes her position, sits adjacent him to give unflinching gazes.

'What is the matter with you woman?! Why are you acting like an illiterate? Is this how to solve the problem? Will you be quiet and return to your seat, please?', he points in the direction of a space she left empty.

'Allow me to talk, let me deal with this man', she gets more infuriated, walking to her seat.

'We have a proof against him, so why should we worry ourselves?'

Segun shifts in his seat uncomfortably. *What do you mean by that? Who is his witness? Who saw me take him away?* His mind is not in much doubt before the truth is revealed.

'Only last week, his wife located our house to expose his evil deeds. He used his friend and God will judge him', Mrs. Ogundare yells and points an accusing finger at him.

'Who? Soronje', Segun's eyes flick from face to face, hoping someone would respond to him. Instead, she hisses irritably.

'Look, Segun, it's no more a secret. Your wife told us everything you did.'

'Me? That's impossible. Please, don't listen to her'.

'Okay. You know what? We will have to involve the police because somebody's life is at stake', he relaxes in the sofa, examining his fidgety moves.

'And to spare our time, we have to do it right now'. Mrs.

Ogundare pulls out her phone. 'I will call them right away'. She dials the number.

'Yes, ride on. He is not confessing the truth'.

Segun rises from his seat, begins to pace around the room, tiredly. *God, why me? What have I done to deserve this? Is it sinful to help a friend in need? Despite knowing me for decades, they still believed a false accusation. What do I do now?*

He makes a sharp turn towards the door and gives it a slight push. He feels Ogundare's penetrating eyes on him. Silence pervades the room; he is ill at ease. He feels an impulse to come back to earth, considering their belief that he sincerely harmed their son. Trying to dissuade them is inconsequential when the police are already involved. He knows them so well- he will be handled as a thief before he gets to their station. Despite the pain he feels in his heart, he swears at the same time, never to have anything to do with Dayo again.

'Hello? Are you on your way?', Mrs. Ogundare asks with a voice loud enough to raise the dead. Straight away, he turns around to give a superficial look. He wonders how she will feel when the truth finally emerges. Will she still accept him as her son as the old time or never have the face to talk to him again? What about his supposed fatherly figure that would push him through hell and high water to get his biological son back. The harm is already done, he knows. But in the midst of his sinking feelings lies the conviction that, he will be castigated for his honesty and goodwill.

'Okay sir. Please follow the direction I gave you in the morning. We are expecting you. Thank you', her face cracks into a faithless smile of gratification. Her husband sits like a statue, blinks like a glaucoma victim. He doesn't know what else to do until the police arrive.

Segun prepares for his hard luck, an imminent agony he never expected anytime in his life. Sooner, he may be put behind bars for his false confession. He peers through the window all the time, sits on a couch to wear his shoes. Soronje's angry face crosses his mind. What more does she have up her sleeve after kicking her out of his life? He looks forward to that but certainly, no condition is around forever. *No condition is permanent. I will be out of this and I will help no more.*

18

M EGHAN STORMS INTO MERCY'S edifice, fanning herself
with a newspaper she got from a grocery store.
Making her ascent of a spiral staircase to the balcony,
she reminisces her festivity when she hits upon the
unprecedented step to win her husband's heart forever.
She was full of the joys of spring, glad to have exorcised
the unhappy thought of losing him to another woman. For
sure, it worked. Life felt so good for them in the United
States, forming a happy family under her stringent control.
At the moment, she is disillusioned by two unobjectionable
reasons causing her inopportune visit in Africa. One,
Mercy's refusal to proffer a solution to the problem. And
two, her expediency leading her into their present situation.

When she visited her two days ago, an argument
supervened- Mercy obstinately refused to help. And it went
on for the next one hour. Only her husband's arrival ended
the conversation, since he is kept in the dark. She had no
choice than to leave and wait for another day. On a day like
this when it's time to talk, she has to be there.

At the time she arrives at her destination, the doors are
wide opened. She takes a few steps in slowly, tiredly, hoping

to clap her eyes on her sister or her newly delivered baby. No trace of them. They should be indoors, somewhere.

'Mercy', she walks into her bedroom, gazes around at disorderly items thrown up and down, the smell of menthol in the air. *Is she hiding from me? She must have* seen *me coming.* She stamps her feet, begins to run out of patience.

'Mercy!', she shouts out her name, infuriated. If she decides to hide this time, it means she meant what she said the last time. That she won't help to restore her husband to health is an unfathomable conception she needs to explain. She wants her support-she knows all about everything-their whole deal.

'What is with you? Why are you acting in a strange manner?', Mercy appears from the guest room. She has been there for over an hour, trying to clean up for a visitor she expects at dusk. She pulls the door close and pads across the dining room to the living room.

'Sit down. Why are you standing like a stranger?', she yawns and stretches her body. She looks over her shoulder to study her mood. She stands still.

'No, I am okay', Meghan passes her tongue over her dry lips, tries to conceal her burning rage.

'Well, if that pleases you, it's alright', she takes her seat, still yawning. She wears a grim look, knowing why she visits.

'Mercy, I have returned to plead with you to- '.

'Hold it there! I told you there is no solution to his problem. That's what he suffers for being a traitor. He betrayed you'.

'You are not in position to judge him. You are not God.

Oh God!'. She holds her head miserably. By the time she drops her hand, she receives a bombshell.

'Mercy, all you offered is a cruel kindness. You didn't help me in any way. You ruined his life and mine too'.

'How? How is it cruel? Tell me how I'm cruel to you?', she rises to her feet, prepares to return to her tasks. She has a lot of chores to complete before her other kids arrive from school. She remembers she left beans cooking in the kitchen. That should be ready in less than one minute and a pile of laundry waits for her care.

'Mercy-don't walk out on me', she slaps her bag on the sofa.

In her moment of quietude, Mercy walks back in the room, wearing a fake smile. The prospects of her misfortunes occur to her and the smile fades away. She wears a strained look. Her uninspiring mood has undeniably stricken her by a pang of sympathy, not only because of her failed marriage but for her deranged hubby whose hide out has not yet been discovered.

'Forget about him. There is no remedy. You don't want to end up with a lunatic, do you?' she tries to cajole her into pessimism.

'Stop calling him that or I'll involve the police in this!', she fires back, rising from her seat, a finger pointed in her face. Mercy is taken aback. She laughs like a drain, walks away from her. She is upset, cant deny that, but she needs to take it cool before she loses it too.

'Hey- sister, enough of your rant. This is uncalled for-stop ranting', she rejoinders, to her utmost surprise. 'You did the same thing the last time you came, so stop!' her lashes beat against taut lids and flaring eyes. It's time to reciprocate and make her realize why she has no power over their tribulation. She can only lead her to stand not prevent her from falling.

'Oh, really? Seriously? Is that what you gonna say now?'

'Yes, sister, get out of my house, now!', she brushes through her, storms to the door. Next to no time, the wooden artifact swings open. She waves her outside, 'please, leave my house. That's all I can do to help you. I am not following you anywhere to heal his madness. I know nothing about that'.

'You do! He is suffering from the effect of your magic. You are a witch!', she stands still. She won't budge till she finds a solution. Leaving there simply implies her acceptance of guilt. And what becomes of her beloved? He would have to spend the rest of his life in the situation. Never!

She looks behind her and slumps in the sofa, 'I'm going nowhere! You must find a way out of this'. At this point, Mercy is at a loss what to do. She pulls a long breath, considers her relationship with her and slams the door shut.

'You know what? I will involve our parents in this', she saunters into the kitchen to recuperate from her lost temper. Her hands fall on the ladle, then a glass cup and straight to the faucet. She is disoriented, doesn't know what to do till she leaves. However, her intuition presages handling the issue cautiously. Her eyes fall on a street light across the road, through a glass window for a moment and she puffs some distressing air. Her self-guilt was quick to set in. How bad is his situation right now? Her doggedness creates a glow of danger prowling around them. Is her marriage over again? How is she going to help him now?

She sneaks through the door and catches Meghan crying. Her head is lowered- she quivers with pain and fear.

'Oh God! Why me? Why did I confide in my sister. She led me astray'. She can't believe her ears, won't accept her conviction. Did she just say that? *Oh my! What did I get myself into?*

Mercy opts to calm herself first before calming her worried sister. Two wrongs don't make a right, and as a sister, she is nurtured to look out for her burdened sibling. She folds her arms and rests on the wall for a moment, waiting to make up her mind. Finally, she walks up to her, an inexpressible stiffness felt around her chest.

'It's okay. He will be fine. He will recover, trust me', she wraps a supportive arm around her, sits on the arm of the sofa.

'I need you to help him. He can't recover without your support. Please, help. Help him-', she looks up pleading, eyes filled with tears. For once, since she pleaded for her help, she reasoned out the role she would have played retracing her step and finding a cure to his illness. But, is she responsible for his problem? She deems it fit to talk it over with her, hit the nail on the head.

'Darling sister', she squeezes her arm, draws close. Her eyes speed to the clock then back to the kitchen. It's about time her family unites for dinner. Besides, she plans to get her baby's milk from a grocery store after cooking. She has to wrap up their discussion as quick as possible. *I need to get her out of my house-quick!*

'We know nothing about his plight. I know much about our men than you do. Listen to me-', she interrupts as she tries to explain. Her mouth hangs half opened.

'He deliberately retuned to his ex. He probably is faking so you can get over it and just- divorce him'.

Is this true? Is it possible he planned it out the way it goes? *Can I trust you? What happens to all the steps you made me take?* Meghan cocks her head, reasoning, digesting her deduction.

'I don't think he can do that. No- no- I don't believe that', she shakes her head, rejecting her shocking supposition. Her fingers unconsciously intertwines, head lowered in absent thought. Mercy looks away confused. Her reflections reform and she comes up with a new idea.

'Sister, what we did was only to attach him to you. We magically made him yours forever, but he ruined it'.

'How? How do you mean?'

She prepares her mind for what else to say then replies, 'he isn't faithful to you. God exposed him and he-'

'Enough! I have to go', Meghan rises and hurries to the door. She follows but before she utters a word, she is out of the apartment. *Finally, I can breathe. Now, I have my peace.* She locks her door and hurries to the kitchen, prepared to pick up where she left off the care of her family. Nothing takes that away from her ever-not even a hurting sister. Watching her drive off her garage, she wonders why she can be unwise to entrust her love life with someone that detests her so much- her worst unknown enemy on earth. *Gosh! How much she places herself as an overlord over all of us. Meghan this- Meghan that. She is the richest, most beautiful, most influential. You can't lead me in marriage, trust me. You will forever fail in that. Dayo is gone, the next man will still be gone, and you will remain lonely forever. I swear.*

19

M RS. WILLIAMS IS PERTURBED by the cheerless news her daughter just disclosed to her only two minutes ago. For a moment, she gazes at her sullenly. Never in her fifty-five years has she envisioned such a hard luck. Today, she admits she is the saddest woman on earth- a failed mother. She rises from the couch she occupies, fixes her with a fiery stare. Her eyes travel from her waning legs to a skinny body sparsely covered with faded dungaree and up towards her belly. She tries covering up with twined fingers. *What a disgrace!* For allowing infatuation to encroach her educational life, she is urged by an impulse to disown her. What else could have curbed a bad patch in a girl's academic achievement and blissful marriage? She is always there for her to provide for all her needs. She understands that, for all she has done to support her, her predicament isn't attached to insufficiency leading young girls to shotgun marriages. Most girls of her age are preoccupied with detrimental thought of getting material gains from men for illicit affairs. A larger girl's population fall victims of pre-marital affairs with married men for financial returns. But for this situation stimulating unlikely suspicion, she hasn't been caught in the act before. Whoever was involved with her must be someone special she needs to know.

'Labi, who is this man', she asks the second time. When she asked what led her to the situation after the disclosure, she smiled impishly and said she loves him. What does she know about love? If she truly narrated the circumstances leading to the absence of her father, she would have chosen to be unmarried forever or perhaps hate the men folks for the rest of her life. Many a time, she tells the same credible story of a nonexistent Mr. Williams tripping to his village and the calamity claiming his life. Is that true? No, he's still very much alive. He only deserted her with two kids and followed another woman he loves more. Whenever Labi sings the praises of her father, she smiles and prays she doesn't stumble across his type. So, what is her situation now? Is she in the same trouble? She gets more apprehensive than when the conversation just began.

Mrs. Williams sighs again. She returns her heavy gaze to her daughter who appears more worried than she seems to be. Why? All she needs at this time is a vital information.

'Labi, who put you in the family way? Is it a ghost?', she advances towards her, makes to attack her.

'No. it's my friend, and-'

'Really? Without marriage? And you just called him your friend. Haven't you put me in trouble?' she explodes. Within the next five seconds, she infers. The best answer is finding him before he denies. Rebuttal of pregnancy is very common in the society as most unlucky girls are left to parent a child with the support of her family. Science and technology makes it easy with the DNA test, only if it is within their means. Who loses in the end? A neglected pregnant girl or her fugitive boyfriend?

'Wait a minute. Is he aware?' she asks a pensive question.

'No, I wasn't-sure. I –'.

'You- be quiet!. Get up and let's go there right now. We have to find him today and tell him. I just hope he accepts- I hope so!' she stares down at her with all the seriousness in the world. Labi scratches her head, shifts from side to side, falls silent and uneasy. Just then, she admits that he isn't truly aware. Come to think of it, is she inclined to disclose the news to him with her mother on her side? She is grown enough to handle the situation herself. But is everything alright? She smells something unusual veiling behind the secret. If there wasn't trouble, shouldn't they be proud to announce the good news to her first? She is grown enough for childbirth but only in the right way. *Is he unpresentable or abnormal?* It is the greatest time she must stand up to support her daughter, avert a shameful denial. It's surprising how arrogant women like her end up after making fun of disadvantaged girls. Many times, she recollects, boasting to friends and family how responsible her daughter is. How will she revert this impending disgrace creeping up on her? Will they run into hiding? Now, she handles the matter more seriously than before. Like greased lightning, she stands up, looks straight at her and screams.

'You are pregnant, and you don't know the father?! Why haven't you told him before?'

'He-'

'He what?' she raises a harsh finger at her, gets terribly demanding for the first time. Labi sighs, gathers her thoughts together, deciding what to say first. This is the time she must say the truth. She toys with her fingers for a couple of seconds, sighs again, her face enwrapped in grief.

'He has something, something akin to insanity. He is suffering from-'

'Madness? Oh I'm in trouble', she wraps her arms around her head, falls in the chair. Nevertheless, she is quick to present her plan.

'I will leave here. I will hide somewhere. I'm so sorry'.

Mrs. Williams is depressed. She sits stone-faced, her hands still around her head. Her minds races to tens of solutions and steps they must take instantly to evade being degraded in the society.

'Get up now! We must find his family. Go and change into something nicer and take me there. Hurry- hurry', she hurries into her room biting he finger, lamenting terribly.

Labi rises expressionless, stomps into her room. Once she was happy as a lark, getting her heart's desire, and at present, she saddles her beloved with a crisis to fiercely have him forever. Their ingrained affair subsequently leads to a mere wishful thinking. She wishes he hadn't hit the glorious offer that wipes smiles off their faces. They were happy together until Meghan emerges in their lives. She weighs up the cause and effect silently and feels stupid, latching onto Soronje's help.

'Labi!' Mrs. Williams calls from the living room.

'Mum- I will join you soon', she changes into an outfit in haste.

'You better do. I don't want us to get there in the evening. I want them to look at me clearly. They can't put my daughter in the family way and deny it', she shouts from the belly of her room.

'Yes mum', she slips on a sky-blue chiffon blouse over a pair of skinny jeans, pulls her scarf then packs her ruffled hair in a sudden rush of anxiety. Now, she finds herself making a choice between two equally undesirable alternatives: being responsible for Dayo's disappearance like Segun or having a fatherless child. Her rival, Meghan, is above suspicion. She visited the ward only once and never called again for his unchallenged loss of memory. She has finally fallen for her sister's persuasion- and prepares to return to the United States. What is her fate? *Today, I have to begin a lifelong journey with him, involving his family. That's my wish- has always been my wish. I would have been the happiest right now.*

20

IT'S A GRAND OCCASION in the month of May. Several familiar people in a similar pattern of blue lace and burgundy head wears are in attendance, flanked by big canopies, seated on white plastic chairs. Pleasurable aroma of delightful meals fill the air, plates knock heads, ecstatic voices filter through a thunderous music. Still in party spirit, some sway to frequently swapped music while others help themselves to nice treats. It isn't over. Twenty minutes after, more people appear and exchange pleasantries amidst permeating noise in a blissful environment.

'Welcome. Why didn't you arrive early for this event?', a curvy lady asks a new attendant.

'My wife delayed me. She compelled me to attend another party with her in the morning', he takes a vacant seat opposite her, looking around to catch a glimpse of the celebrant. His eyes finally rest on her as she attends to a guest. Having noticed him from afar, she gives no attention, whatsoever. He knows he owes her an apology for his uninformed lateness and most importantly, his failure to fulfil yet another promise. Only two weeks ago, he moved heaven and earth with empty promises to provide chairs and canopies bright and early. He failed after its been ruled out of her budget, banking on his pledges. Although it's late but now it dawns on her that the success or failure of his plans depends on him.

'Where is the celebrant?', he asks still looking around, pretending not to have seen him.

'She is busy with other guests in her bedroom. She just left here', she smiles.

'Okay, I have to see her immediately', he rises from the seat, walks past a small group, bunching up for prayers and enters a spacious yard. Every minute, he bumps into familiar people, halts and greets them, feeling a twinge of shame and distrust. It's been a long time he sets his eyes on them or even thought of visiting, owing to his unmet promises. The occasion seems to invite them all to confront him, especially Mr. Ezekiel who he promised to gift a bike to run his farm business. To avoid his pressure and persuasion, he has long stopped visiting his neighborhood- about two years ago.

'What?! Johnson! Is this you? Am I seeing clearly? Ezekiel's mouth hangs open in amazement.

'Good afternoon sir, I just-'

'Johnson! Is this you?', he cuts in, still bewildered. In their last conversation, barely six days ago, he lied he travelled overseas. *Why is the moon out in the day?*

'I can explain'

'No way, you still failed today, didn't you?' with a wave, he ignores him and walks away. His face flickers with contempt. How can he make them understand him or reason out why he fails all the time if no one tries to listen? *I think they are just too selfish. They care only about themselves and not others.* He always has the zeal to help but somewhere down the line, something comes up, causing financial restraint. In many cases, this has led to misconception between him and his wife. The bone of contention is how much hatred he gets from the ones he dissatisfied. For Ezekiel, he really proposed to get the motorbike, but his son suddenly fell sick and he needed money to pay hospital bills. Now, nothing makes him believable.

He continues his journey to the room, thinking of what the celebrant would say on his recent displeasure. She would probably say all Ezekiel just said to him.

No one is aware of his presence at the entrance. The celebrant breast feeds her newborn, her gaze fixed on him. For a couple of minutes, he glues to the wall, drinking in the wonders of nature, picturing the great transformation of a tiny baby into a fully grown man like him one day. All cuddled up, he is enshrouded in his shawl, suckling eagerly, eyes closed, pink tiny nose turned up. He smiles, then proceeds inside the room.

'Good afternoon', he greets shamefaced.

'Welcome', Labi's mum breathed. She returns her gaze to Mrs. Ogundare almost immediately. On his matter, she decides to save her breathe, not nag and yank all day on immaterial liar like him. He appreciates not touching on it, but his conscience wouldn't let him be till he reverts to the issue once more.

'Stop! That's a by- gone. Get yourself a seat', Mrs. Williams deters him from explicating. She has spent the whole day talking at her grand kid's christening. She looks forward to arriving home and going off to sleep. *Please excuse me.*

After feeding her baby, Mrs. Williams collects it and

set to her duties before taking her leave. She has to bathe him, and his mum then hand them over to Mrs. Ogundare. Other chores are carried out by Labi herself.

'Don't worry. You are tired. I will take care of that', Mrs. Ogundare collects the sleeping baby from her and returns him to his crib.

'Alright thank you very much. I'll be here first tomorrow morning.', she gets her bag.

'I think I should be going too. My wife will be expecting me', Mr. Johnson tucks a crisp thousand note in Labi's hand, folds her fists to cover it.

'Thank you so much. Say hello to your wife and kids', Labi follows them to the door.

'Do stay with the baby. I will see them off. And I'll be right back', her mother- in- law leads the way and beckons to the baby.

Labi walks towards the room. As she shuffles across the corridor, where her beloved's room is situated, she overhears two people whispering about something and stops over. She moves a few steps closer to eavesdrops.

'Now, what do we do about this predicament? Last year, you were raving mad. And this year?', he pauses, sulks then continues bitterly, 'You are a bat. You can't see anyone'. A rather too long silence follows, then a louder sulking sound is audible.

'Father- I don't know what I did to merit this kind of punishment. Oh God, it's beyond my understanding', Dayo says crying.

'Oh no son- stop crying. God will heal you. He saved you the first time and will still come to your rescue this time. He will never forsake you', he consoles him.

Labi drops her hands from the wall, walks off the spot. She makes her way back to her room, to rejoin her child. No one is with him; her mother-in-law is still outside with her mum. From the window, she hears their hearty conversation about Johnson. She listens disinterestedly, then rises to pull it close. David, her newly christened baby is asleep, all wrapped up in a lengthy shawl. Silently, she watches him- he looks so adorable. He is a perfection of love and life except for the time he is born. *Now, what is my gain? He's back in Africa to achieve what? It's like driving him in more trouble. Yes, I love him but not in this state. I think I'm responsible for all his woes in life.*

She sinks into her bed, laid her back down thinking, her eyes on the ceiling. What now? Is she going to live the rest of her life through this agony? Is it the same charm that claimed his sight? If that is the case then all is vanity- vanity upon vanity. *Curse Soronje!*

'Labi,

'Yes?', Labi turns around to meet his steady gaze. He fixes his eyes on the same spot, takes a few steps forward. He can't see anything, only throws his hands in the air for direction.

'Wait- let me come for you', she hurries towards him.

'It's alright. I just want to see- no, feel my son and you too, before we all go to bed', he holds her hand, squeezes a little bit, fondly. He can't explain the happy feeling he has around her.

'Oh- please come with me. The baby is here', she walks him to his crib, smiling- her attention wholly on the newborn.

'Does he have my face', he runs his hand over his face, feels his tender nose in his palm then his soft lips. He licks him thinking it's food. He smiles at this. Labi has a hard face.

'Yes, he looks exactly like you', she responds wondering why his eyes are wide open and he can't see anything.

'I can feel his nose is pointy', he turns to find a seat. She helps him to her bed.

'I wanted to attend his christening, but mummy stopped me'.

'I understand'.

'And- how are you?', he searches for her next to him, swaddles her with a protective arm, a happy smile on his face. Labi's face drops. She knows, that for a long time to come, she won't come to term with the virulent guilt eating deep in her soul, probing her heedless decision. Who suffers the pain now?

She cries silently. Not seeing or having a clue of what transpires beside him, he smiles on. He caresses her arm and accidentally touches her wet face. His smile fades away, all at once. He looks curious.

'Labi why are you crying? Are you okay?', he rubs her face, wipes the tears off.

'No, I'm okay. I just remembered our good old time together', she lies, preventing a word about her transgression. The saint having the gumption to disclose her secret is gone. He won't ever find him again after he was jailed for three months before he was found.

'The good old time? Yes, you and I without this problem. I know but do you believe we can still have that again?', he waits for her response, but she chooses to be silent for the rest of the night. He knows she is afraid, doesn't know what more will surface. He is in position to inspire her, purge her of all ill thoughts about their misery. He knows it is tough, nonetheless he will try. Not willing to give up hope on his breakthrough, he strokes her arm, smiling and gazing at a wrong direction.

'Darling, the good old time shall return with wealth and joy, believe me. Stop crying honey. We shall be happy together forever'. Labi sighs at the mention of forever. Is she ready for this adventurous journey? Maybe yes or no- she is confused.

To gladden him, she gives a forced answer. And Dayo senses this, 'do you still love me, regardless of all I have done to hurt you? Please, forgive me'.

'Yes, I -I have forgiven you. I still love you so much- with all my heart', again, she feels he same guilt clutching at her heart, and moves closer. She wraps her arms around him, leans her head on his chest. The future holds their destinies, can tell what happens next, good or bad. Yet, she is afraid.

'I love you too and I will always do'.

She is pushed to express her pain and seek for forgiveness too, confess all her sins so peace will reign again in her heart. Easy as it sounds, it is sorely difficult. What about his parents? How will they react to this?

'I am yours forever now and nothing takes me away from you again. Not money, love, or anything you can imagine in a man's life', he assures still smiling. This is the only time she will appraise the magic that brings her dream back home, away from avaricious hands of false affection. For all other reasons, it is bad.

'Yes, fiercely mine forever'.

Love bade me welcome: yet my soul drew back,
Guilty of dust and sin.
But quick-eyed love, observing me grow slack
From my first entrance in,
Drew nearer to m, sweetly questioning
If I lacked anything.

George Herbert.

Printed in the United States
by Baker & Taylor Publisher Services